Anna 2026

First Printing, 2012

ISBN 978-0-9873693-3-8

Somnium Books

www.somniumbooks.com

To those who believed in me, my heartfelt thanks.
To those who doubted, my eternal gratitude.

This book is dedicated to the raven-haired beauty of my
dreams; may she haunt them forever.

Anna 2026

Lucas Morgan

Prologue

A drop of rain. Another, and then another, thumped into my closed eyelid and trickled into the corner of my mouth. I was cold, my limbs heavy and numb. I thought I was close to death, could feel my life hanging by a thread. I whispered a prayer to the universe to take me, for my body to give up, to let go; but still I lingered, hoping that the burning pain in my chest and the agony in my back were part of the dying process. Or perhaps I was already dead and this would be my hell, bent against a tree and shivering for all eternity.

I kept my eyes closed and breathed out long and deep, praying it would be my last; and sobbing as my chest rose of its own accord, my bleeding lung gurgling full of air. I held tight to the cold weight on my chest and kept my eyes closed, my back near-fused into a curve, the bark of the tree cutting into my shoulders.

Jesus, man, die; just let go and die.

I drifted in and out of wakefulness, pain and the weight held tight to my chest my world entire. It was dark, that much could be told without opening my eyes; distant thunder rolled, whether marking the storm's retreat or advance impossible to tell. Each time I lost consciousness I hoped never to return; and each time I woke to the same agony, and a world slowly graying. Dawn had come, and with it my senses awakened.

I opened my eyes and wailed like a madman. The sound echoed through the forest until my voice croaked to silence and I slowly pushed myself to my feet.

1.

"Hey you sure you're not coming? Hey, Riley."

I pulled myself away from the office window, surprised that I hadn't heard the warehouse floor manager stomp up the stairs. Ben filled the doorway with his bulk, ledger under arm and mug of black coffee in hand. A small light at the top of the stairs cast his shadow over the office. We shared a few moments of awkward silence, broken only by cars on the street below. Their headlights sent beams arcing through the office; the dark all the deeper for their passing.

I shook my head slightly, his words beyond comprehension.

"You do remember you said you'd see it with me?"

"Oh yeah, the movie," I mumbled, glancing over my shoulder to the window, and the darkening street outside.

"So I take it that's a no then?" he remarked, draining the last of his coffee and stifling a yawn with the back of his hand.

I ran a hand though my hair and nodded, eyes to the floor, "Yeah ... no I cant. There's a bunch of work I need to catch up on."

"Man you two really need to get back to your old rule; sign off when Ben does and go home. You guys cant keep staying here till midnight trying to outdo one another. It's just a job remember. Hey where is Anna anyway? I haven't seen her since yesterday."

I avoided his eyes and feigned indifference with a yawn. "Oh she had some things to catch up on. Hey about the movie, I'll come next time for sure."

"Yeah right, you never come. You aren't worried about the shipment are you? They always get through customs. Just let them play their little game. You know what they're like when it's coming direct from China. We could be smuggling in spies or something."

My smile was forced as I sat at my desk and started poking at the keys; the data I was pretending to enter nothing but gibberish on the screen.

It felt as if hours passed before he finally conceded with a raised hand, the movement flicking shadow across the room, "Alright, I can tell when I'm not wanted. I'm going to see it anyway, it better be as good as you said. Oh and don't forget, the alarm doesn't arm itself. If I get here in the morning and find this place wide open like that again I'm telling her."

I looked across to Anna's' work space, empty since yesterday.

"She'd kick your ass for it, and then mine for not telling her sooner. See you tomorrow."

"Huh? Oh, yeah tomorrow."

He stood in the doorway a moment longer, watching me as I typed more garbled text. When he finally left I let out a sigh and slumped forward, a hand held to my temple. I checked my cell again and the knot in my stomach tightened; none of the messages I'd sent my wife, Anna, had been answered.

I pushed my chair back and vomited between my feet.

Moments later I returned to the window, cell clutched in hand, and prayed to a god I didn't believe in for some sign of my wife.

· · ·

I shouldered my way through the thronging streets, my eyes darting from one face to another in the passing crowd. The night was reaching its zenith and still the city teemed, the multitude going about their concerns under plasma billboards flashing government warnings and gaudy advertisements.

The hum of electric motors mingled with the voices of thousands, the cacophony reaching deafening proportions whenever I passed yet another over-hanging plasma blaring this week's top single; the screens flashing naked, writhing bodies, the tune both catchy yet indistinguishable from a hundred others the mob once favoured.

A flash of dark hair across the street caught my eye, I was halfway across the road when the woman turned and crushed the spark of hope her glossy hair had borne. The crowd swallowed her a second after, a screech of tyres and blare of horn sent me scrambling back onto the teeming sidewalk. The driver screamed insults after me, but I was deaf to all, my eyes never ceasing to rove from one face to another, as if I might know if any of the passing strangers had laid eyes on my Anna, and would somehow lead me to her. I found no such succour and pushed on, my destination within sight at the end of the block.

The small retro clothing store was packed. The women tearing through racks of jackets and shirts were as frantic as the remixed rock that blared throughout; the chaotic environment whipping the shoppers into a spending frenzy. It was the same atmosphere of passionate consumerism that had driven me to wait outside a month ago, while Anna picked up a jacket she'd ordered.

I recognised the girl she'd dealt with; she moved from one customer to another, tthe metal studs and luminescent implants under her skin gave her a bizarre, otherworldly appearance. I weaved through the throng of chattering women and tapped her on the shoulder. She ignored me, and stood with arms crossed, eyeing off a pink haired girl who'd thrown on a patched flannel shirt and was awaiting her appraisal.

Her voice was as manic as the music thumping through the store.

"That's it girl, def the one. It's original, worn in 95, comes with pics of the concert where the patches were bought. Just roll … "

I tapped her shoulder again and cleared my throat. She sighed and turned, her face a brief scowl that brightened when she recognised me; Anna had spent a lot of money in the store.

"Hey cutie, where's the wife?"

She was already scanning the store for Anna when I pulled her attention back to me. It was then she noticed the state I was in, I hadn't showered in three days, nor eaten. She gave me a quick up and down, her brow knitting.

"Have you seen my wife? Has she been here?" My voice trembled slightly, reason enough for her scowl to deepen as she took a small step back.

"No … not since she picked up the jacket. You ok man? Serious, you good?"

I was already leaving the store, ignoring her and the rest of the now silent women, their eyes boring into my back until the current of the sidewalk swept me away.

A temporary pocket of calm in the river of people gave me space to check my cell. The reprieve was short-lived, the crowd jostling me as I blinked away tears and searched for a message or missed call. Though I knew by now that there would be no answer I tried anyway, scanning the streets until I reached her voicemail. I hung up quickly, lest the sound of her voice recording brake me.

Shoulders struck mine, passers-by raged at me for blocking the path, but still I stood frozen, contemplating calling the authorities and reporting my wife missing; the thought sent a wave of nausea through the pit of my stomach. I put my cell away and pushed on, the city swallowing me, as it had my Anna.

· · ·

"That's it, Riley, don't go running off now."

I gasped for air and struggled to rise. My throat constricted again as two dark-suited men held me down on the couch in our living room. One of them twisted my neck and pressed a beefy forearm into my throat, allowing me enough air to stay alive and little more.

A third man stalked around our small apartment, running his hand through short-cropped orange hair while he grinned and chewed manically on gum. He stopped in front of the bookshelf and picked up a photo of Anna and I, mumbling under his breath and sniggering. The men put more weight on me, bearing down with all their strength as I growled and struggled to rise.

Orange-hair dragged a chair from the small dining table behind him, the legs scratching into the glossy floorboards as he stalked towards me and sat opposite. The same grin still mocked me. His eyes were black with engorged pupils, as were those of the two men restraining me. Orange-hair was young, no more than twenty-five. The arrogance that came with having power and youth emanated from him like a noxious vapour.

"You know I can put you away for that," he said, eyes glued to the photo, "assaulting an Intervention Officer is an automatic six months, Riley — big trouble now."

He flipped the photo around — my arm was draped over Anna's shoulder, the park behind us gold in the autumn sun. She was beautiful, the sinking sun lighting her glossy black hair, her dark eyes full of warmth; a primal goddess radiating life next to me — though most looked plain and grey beside her.

I was exhausted, my mind in tatters. I should have laid still, but the sight of him holding a picture of my wife drove me into a frenzy; and though they were big men, they were hard-pressed to keep me pinned.

"Bit out of your league, isn't she, Riley?" he sneered, showing the picture to his colleagues.

"Told you, boys — primo. What a waste." He sighed dramatically and dropped the photo to the floor, before leaning back with both hands behind his head; he looked at me as if I were rotten food just spat out.

"Jesus, I'm sick of you people! I can't remember the last time I slept. You know how many of these we've done in the past three days, Riley? How many is it now?"

The man choking me shrugged, the movement taking some weight off the side of my throat.

I gasped a lungful of air, "Where is she?"

"Sorry?" Orange-hair mocked, leaning in with a hand cupped behind his ear, a gaudy Rolex rattling down his wrist.

I tried to speak again, but the man bore down again as Orange-hair pulled a small silver tube from his pocket. "Why, she's in the same place you're going, Riley."

The room turned blue as he shone the small light into my eyes. A moment later a green light flashed on the side of the device. He scowled and flashed the light again, this time holding it to my eyes for twice as long. The same green light disappointed him a second time.

"Looks like you've been a good boy then."

He continued chewing as he spoke, his eyes roving around the living room before he leaned in to within an inch of my face.

"Makes you wonder why she took it without telling you, doesn't it?" he said, with a bemused half grin. His swollen pupils searched my face as if he cared what my answer might be.

"A man should know what his wife is doing, don't you think?"

The forearm pressed down as I wheezed and shook my head slightly. Orange-hair rolled his eyes and leapt to his feet, the chair crashing to the floor behind him. "Christ!

You know I wish once, just once, that one of you fucking people would admit what you've done. It's always the same shit — 'I haven't taken anything, — please, you have to believe me — there's been a mistake'— blah blah blah."

He absentmindedly stepped on the photo, his immaculately polished shoe ground Anna and I into the floor as he looked around the apartment straightening his jacket. A few deep breaths seemed to calm him, he nodded to himself before looking back to me, never once ceasing his assault on the gum in his mouth.

"Well, let's get it over with then. I'll tell you what, Riley, we can make a deal. I'm going to read something to you, and when I'm done you're going to sign some paperwork. You do that and I'll let you off. We can just forget that swing you took at me. We'll all just get on with our lives with no fuss. How's that sound?"

He pulled a small black book from his pocket and opened it with a deft flick. "I don't really need this anymore," he said, with a glance at the worn book, "but rules is rules. Thank Christ they're phasing this shit out. Not long now and the whole system changes. No more interventions to smooth things over. It's going automated. You're lucky to be getting so much special treatment, Riley. I don't know what we're going to do when they pull us off the streets. I think its important for people to have that human contact, don't you?"

His words were a blur, his chewing manic.

I groaned and fought to escape the two men; but they were strong, their grip iron.

Orange-hair grinned and stuffed the book into his pocket. "You know what — let's see if I can do it from memory, hey?"

He rubbed his hands together and spat the gum out of the side of his mouth, then righted the chair to sit opposite again.

"It is with great regret, that I, Jason Whiting, of the Department of Intervention, along with agents Tyler and McKinnon, inform you that at 21:30 this evening, your former wife, Mrs Anna Mitchell Dainon, was found guilty of ingesting a prohibited substance in violation of the Steadfast Act. At 22:00 she willingly renounced her citizenship, and at 23:00 was deported to District Four of the Exclusion Zone."

He clapped his hands and leant back with a wild smile. "Not bad, hey?"

He popped another piece of gum in his mouth and started chewing viciously for a few seconds.

"Mr. Dainon, it is important you understand that the severity of your wife's punishment is proportionate to the danger she posed to the public around her. The Department of Immigration has acted to protect your fellow citizens from harm … Christ! It goes forever. You don't need to hear it all, right?"

If the men had released me then I would have killed him, but they kept me twisted and crushed while their peer revelled in his performance. He soon finished his oratory and slammed a small pile of papers onto the coffee table by the lounge.

The two goons seized my hand and steered from one page to another, the arm around my throat constricted every time I resisted.

"Relax Riley, this is going to happen no matter what. That's it, right here. Jesus hold him! This one is to acknowledge that you witnessed your wife ingesting a prohibited substance on multiple occasion and that you requested an intervention."

He laughed and lightly cuffed one of the men holding me with the bundle of documents. "Ease up you savages. He does have to breathe you know! Now, where were we, ah ha, last one. This one waves your right to appeal on behalf of your wife and —can't forget this part. See, it says you understand that if you pursue the matter you can be imprisoned for up to five years without trial. I like that bit."

My face was wet with tears by the time it was over, my throat raw and my strength spent.

"Good boy, Riley! I'll leave your copies here. Make sure you read these pamphlets as well. Lots of info on the free therapy you can get, and the widower's assistance program and all that shit. They love throwing money at you people."

He stood chewing with eyes wide as he pulled another small item from his coat and waved it in front of my face.

"You see this? Taser — one of the new sonic ones. If I have to use this you'll probably piss yourself. So you just sit there like a good boy."

The two men slowly loosened their grip on me. I gasped a lungful of air and lay still, knowing they were ready to crush me again should I give them cause.

"Good boy, no sense making things worse for yourself. Hey, this is nice," Orange-hair snatched Anna's blue scarf from the couch beside me. I'd found it crumpled on the floor two days ago, and had been sleeping with it on the couch when the door had burst open. An image of her flashed through my mind, sitting next to me while we watched a movie; 'making knitting cool', as she put it.

"I might keep this, Riley. It's my girlfriend's birthday in a few days and I haven't got her shit," he said, kneading the soft material in his large square hand and laughing with the two men.

I exploded from the couch and screeched like a lunatic as I struck him a crushing blow to the jaw. He dropped instantly, with me on top of him. I closed my hands about his neck and squeezed, his swollen, purpling face all that existed. I was beyond reason, beyond myself. All the powerlessness and rage I had felt for the past three days as I had searched the city for my wife poured into those few seconds of murderous throttling.

A deafening explosion snapped my head to the side. The world burned white, and then I fell into darkness.

2.

"Stop showing off; you've been wearing it for the past week. I get it, I was wrong, you finished it; you're a knitting machine," I said, sitting up in bed and watching as Anna gave her long, dark hair a flick and tied the scarf around her neck.

"Who's showing off? It's cold outside," she grinned, applying lip balm, "You'd notice if you stopped sleeping in."

"I'll confiscate it if you don't behave."

"Come on then, Fatty," she teased, her eyes wide at the dangerous game she played. I leapt from the bed; she squealed and bolted.

"Don't, I'm ready for work," she said with grave seriousness, as I dragged her to the bed. Her pleas fell on deaf ears, her lips glossy and tempting.

"There's no time; I have to open. Ben doesn't know the new code for the warehouse yet. They'll be waiting," she pleaded.

"King Riley demands satisfaction, Lady Anna. His subjects will have to wait." My eyes were hooded slits as I unwound the scarf and pulled her to the bed.

"Anna!"

I sat upright and felt by my side; praying that it had all been some cruel dream, one that would have us both pondering its meaning on our morning walk to the warehouse.

The mattress underneath was thin and unfamiliar. I called to her again, the metallic sound of my voice bouncing back startling me.

"Anna."

I swung my legs over the side of the bed and winced; cold, grated steel bit into my bare feet. My heart began to beat wildly as I ran my hand along the steel walls surrounding me, moving quickly towards a thin line of light on the floor. What small hope the light had borne was crushed when I floundered into another wall of solid metal, the beacon nothing but light coming through a gap millimetres wide where door met floor.

I clawed and pounded against the doorway, screaming for her, for them to let me out, for them to take me to her. Muffled voices of men echoed through the dark, telling me to be silent, threatening death unless I let them sleep in peace. I kept up my assault on the solid steel door, flesh pounding steel, my voice tearing from an already raw throat.

My last sight of her burned vividly in my mind. She hurried across the street as I watched from the office window; her black hair gleaming in the morning sun, her bright blue scarf a slash of sapphire against the deep red of her knee-length coat. And then she was gone.

I groaned and held my face in my hands as I paced through the dark, despair crushing me until I returned to my assault on the door. I screamed her name until my voice was gone, struck steel until my hands were broken and bleeding and my legs collapsed. She fled from me; the mist swallowing her as I reached out, her voice soft and her words a mystery.

. . .

White light stung me to wakefulness, blinding me for a brief moment as it streamed through heavy, half-opened eyelids.

A small beep drew my attention; I rolled my head languidly to the side and watched as fluid filled a clear tube. I followed the stream's progress down the length of plastic and watched it seep into the vein in my wrist, its meaning beyond me. I strained against the thick straps that bound me to the steel table until another beep sounded, though this time distant and small. My hands were tightly bandaged, as was my knee. My eyelids became heavy, too heavy.

Darkness descended.

Anna stood before me, her back turned. She was close, though when I called to her my voice was lost in the void between us. I called to her again and reached out, only for her to fade away; a ghost melting from my grasp. I woke in tears, the waking world screaming in on me as more fluids were pumped into my arm.

I saw no one in the infirmary, though I woke to clean bandages, sometimes tighter than they had been before, my position slightly altered. The cycle went on and on; I lost all concept of time, of day and night. To be conscious was torment, I began to pray for the succour of sleep to take me back to her.

Leave me with her. Let this sleep never end.

. . .

My medicated purgatory ended as mysteriously as it had begun, and I awoke on my side in a small grey cell, half the size of the infirmary. A round light was set deep into the ceiling, weakly illuminating the unadorned room and glinting off the cold, steel walls.

My legs collapsed under me the moment I put weight on them, sending me sprawling across the grated steel floor. My mind was slow, my body heavy and numb, a sedative hangover lingering.

I lay panting on the cold steel, my face pressed against the ridges.

Get up; fucking get up.

But I could not, I lay pathetic and broken, lost in self indulgence. It was many minutes later that I pushed myself to my hands and knees. I stayed on all fours for a few moments, hanging my head, eyes closed. I could have wept, I wanted to. I fought off the rising despair with a growl and pushed myself to a sitting position, leaning my back against the cold steel wall while the room swam.

When my vision finally cleared I sat staring blankly ahead, taking deep breaths in an effort to center myself, to focus and regain my wits. My fists were clenched, nails biting into flesh.

Don't let them beat you. She needs you, you can fix this Riley, you can fix this.

I was halfway to my feet when a loud siren and flash of red from the light in the ceiling filled the room, sending me cringing instinctively. A second later the steel doors slid open with a hiss, a grated steel hallway running past the entrance. In moments it filled with men in dark gray overalls hurrying past my cell. Many glanced in as they passed, whispering amongst themselves.

I noticed I too was dressed the same, and the room began to spin as the magnitude of my situation dawned on me. I would have vomited had my stomach not been empty. Instead my mouth filled with bile as I sank to the floor, ignoring the second siren and flash of red from above. A third siren wailed. I should have pushed myself to my feet and joined the other prisoners, but I couldn't. I sat on the grated floor with head hung as men continued to shuffle by like broken cattle.

The light in the ceiling flashed red a fourth time, a second later my muscles contorted; pain, like none I had ever felt, seared through my body. The electrical current came and went in seconds, my body thrashing beyond control. I was left breathless and trembling, sprawled across the metal floor with saliva running from my mouth, my limbs heavy and foreign. I rolled to my back and glared insolently at the light; again it flashed. Again the current ran through the floor; this time more powerful, causing me to gurgle and shriek involuntarily as I writhed, my limbs flailing.

I lay on my side, staring vacantly at the steel wall, what will I'd preserved now gone.

"Kill me, kill me you soulless bastards," I groaned.

It was a selfish, foolish challenge, one I'm ashamed I made.

I was saved from finding out just how far the little red light would go in our game of chicken by strong hands that grabbed me under the arms and dragged me from the cell.

3.

My saviours hurried away down the hall, muttering under their breath in Spanish as they caught up with their peers. One of them glanced over his shoulder and we locked eyes for the briefest of moments. He was younger than his colleague, probably no more than twenty; though the tattoos and scars gouged across his swarthy face concealed much.

They disappeared quickly down a sloping ramp, leaving me standing on unsteady legs; alone in a long corridor of steel stretching away to my left, revealing more cell doors than I could count. To my right, the cells ended just beyond my own, the ramp sloping steeply out of view. The murmur of hundreds of voices washed into the hallway from wherever it led.

I remained where I was, not willing to descend down the ramp into what I imagined to be waiting. I leaned against the wall, my heart beating in my ears, my mouth dry.

God, let this be a dream, a nightmare. Wake me to her, I beg you.

Another siren and flash of red from above, another light flickering a warning. My legs took me limping down the ramp before I had time to consider defiance, shuffling me away from the pain that would come if I disregarded the light's orders. The slope was steep enough to cause further pain in my knee as I limped along, watched over by evenly-spaced lights in the ceiling. The hum of a hundred conversations filled the empty hall. I continued on with jaw clenched and head high, the sound surrounding me; my stomach knotting as I neared the end of the ramp.

I gasped as the corridor opened up, my eyes darting from one prisoner to another as they walked past the opening. I forced my legs to keep moving as I looked out over the massive auditorium in a daze. A gleaming steel hall stretched hundreds of meters distant, a seamless expanse of moulded metal. Thousands of men milled about like a stirred-up nest of ants under a high ceiling covered in familiar red lights. More ramps, identical to the one I had shuffled down, hinted at a vast network of cells feeding men into this central area. I limped into the multitude, eying the crowd of grey-clad prisoners while I forced myself to keep moving.

Show them nothing. They don't know you.

I kept my eyes distant, and walked with false confidence, returning the gaze of any eyes I met and matching the contempt I saw — the act fooled only the actor. I was a lamb in a lion cage. It was written all over me, easy for the many scowling faces to see as they turned, sporadically, to regard me. I ignored the many sets of eyes, and the occasional hostile comment as the crowd swallowed me.

The smell of fried food wafted through the air, sending my stomach into a fit of gurgling as I wandered aimlessly about. I had eaten nothing since Anna had gone missing — food having been the least of my concerns as I scoured the city for any sign of her. I ignored the painful lurching in my stomach and found an unoccupied seat against one of the walls. I sat, silent and brooding, thinking only of her.

She's out there. I can't be here. I can't be in here.

The hall was vast, the walls and ceiling moulded steel, though still I looked for a possible way out. There seemed no chink in the prison's glinting steel armour. Wherever I was, it had certainly been designed by people smarter and more resourceful than me; built to keep in men more cunning and experienced than I could ever be.

I ceased scanning the high walls and camera-riddled ceiling, defeated in mere moments and hung my head. My plans for a daring breakout melted away, as did my awareness of my surroundings.

Her red gown shimmered even in the dim lighting, stark in the crowd of dark-clad business men and their equally drab female peers she weaved through. Anna radiated life, as she always did; the skin of her bare arms golden brown, her glossy black hair hanging loose down her back.

Others wouldn't see it, but I could tell she would rather be anywhere else.

"You look beautiful, very glamorous," I whispered in her ear, as she stood beside me.

She made a show of rolling her eyes and smoothed out an imaginary crease on her dress. "Don't, I'm way overdressed."

"No, you're not!" I said, nodding towards a young woman in a skimpy black dress across the room. "See – look at her; she's as dressed up as you are and only looks half as good."

I had spent an hour convincing her to wear something elegant, something other than the jeans and shirt she had been trying to get away with, and I wasn't about to let her lose her confidence now.

"Plus," I said, "I need you looking good if you're standing next to me. I feel like James Bond in this suit, and you're the sexy Russian chick that I'll bed in my yacht later tonight."

She raised an eyebrow, "Oh, really? And I suppose you'll be showering me in jewellery in your penthouse after that?"

"Nope, you Bond girls never last. It'll probably be the C.I.A agent over there I'll be showering," I said, nodding towards the young women in the black dress.

She was pinching me before I finished, her dark eyes burning, her lips a hard line. I yelped and squirmed to get away as she dug her claws deeper into the fat at my waist. "Don't worry though, you'll always be my Russian connection," I chuckled, between gasps.

"Go on; keep digging your hole, little man."

"But you never know, maybe we could arrange a meeting; a joint agency operation in the penthouse." I was all set to carry on, but the pain was too much; I yelped and buckled.

"That's what I thought," she said, letting go and sipping her drink while she scanned the crowd.

I rubbed at the burning pain in the small roll of fat that had been growing around my waist these past few months.

"I suppose you'll be wanting another drink then, ma'am?"

"Good boy," she teased.

"You know I'm going to get you back."

She smiled and patted me on the cheek, "Sure you are, pumpkin."

I was grinning as I moved to the busy bar. Anna and I always made a show of giving each other a hard time at parties or other social events; it was our way of hiding our various insecurities. Both of us would have preferred to be at home rather than surrounded by wannabe corporate bigwigs and low-ranking bureaucrats. But our business was growing quickly, and at some point we would need these people. Plus, the drinks were free – and we were both taking full advantage of the cocktail list.

I ordered a whiskey sour and a virgin Mojito, lounging against the bar and watching Anna struggle to make conversation with another couple. I recognised them, they were a little older than Anna and I, edging forty; the man had been in the army before he and his wife started an electronics business. They specialized in the newest gadgetry to come out of Asia, from personal DNA testing equipment to the latest in surveillance and counter-surveillance supplies.

I collected our drinks and made my way back as the couple moved off. I handed Anna hers.

"They asked again. I told them it's not likely," she murmured.

"It's still worth discussing, you know. There are lots of ways we would benefit from joining them; plus they're both nice enough to deal with."

Anna's reply was terse. "I told you, I want to do it on our own; we're growing fast enough. I don't want to have to compromise, and you know that's what will happen."

"It's just a thought. We can talk about it without actually doing it; I'm just throwing ideas around."

She shrugged and sipped at her drink, as did I, the conversation ending there. We were both stubborn and I knew better than to push it.

She finished her drink and left without saying a word, though I barely noticed; I'd become embroiled in a debate with a young political analyst on the war in Iran, which naturally led to the governments not so covert involvement with the resistance fighters in Taiwan and its abandonment of thousands of our soldiers to the Chinese. He was barely out of his teens; but already he spoke as if he knew what was best for the world. His neatly packaged, black-and-white view infuriated me.

I was in the middle of telling him about my two years in China when a burst of laughter across the room caught my attention. I followed the turning heads to see Anna leaning on the bar with her head thrown back. She grabbed an embarrassed waiter and dragged him to the dance floor. I watched, bewildered, as she began flinging the poor boy around. A space was cleared and the music turned up. Others, most of them drunk, joined in until Anna and her captive disappeared into the crowd.

The drinks kept flowing and the music increased in tempo. I left the kid and moved closer to watch Anna, who was still trying to convince the waiter to dance with her. A moment later I rescued the poor boy, who was politely trying to decline Anna's flirtatious invitations.

We made love that night. It hadn't been like that in years. I should have known then; I should have seen it. But I was drunk, and happy to be getting such attention. We went for hours, until I could no longer stay awake; and I drifted off to sleep with her moaning and fondling me in the dark.

She woke me the next morning with the same willingness, though the sparkle had left her eyes and the giggles were gone. I did my best to keep up, but she was insatiable and I begged for rest. She scowled and slapped me lightly across the face. Then she was up and moving around the house; preparing breakfast, cleaning, making calls, getting dressed. A whirlwind of clanking, chattering, frying madness.

I barely managed to get myself out of bed.

I must have seemed deranged as I sat huddled against the wall in the prison, eyes squeezed shut, my one working hand balled and grinding into my temple. I spat and groaned, seeking to erase the guilt that tore at me.

It's your fault, Riley. It's your fault, you should have done something, you should have known.

The aroma of food pulled me from my stupor. A group of men walked past with steaming plastic trays trailing a mouth-watering scent.

My eyes followed the line of men to the source of the irresistible aroma of grease and fried fat. A long bench stretched twenty metres down the hall, behind it toiled near fifty prisoners, serving food and stacking empty trays in gurneys. I held back a moment, unsure of how to proceed, and guilty at the thought of stuffing myself with food.

My hesitation was only momentary, my painful hunger overriding such reservations. I watched a bent old man take a plastic tray from one of the many piles on the front counter. He then shuffled over and presented it to one of the sweating men ladling out food. A few spoons of this and that, some gravy, and he moved away, to be replaced by another prisoner.

I limped over and repeated what I had seen, avoiding eye contact with the man who dumped boiled sausage and peas onto my tray and mumbling thanks out of instinct, which he didn't hear or chose to ignore. I took one of the rubbery gel-forks and shuffled back to my wall space.

The food was quickly gone, my desperate hunger making short work of the small meal. The fork soon dissolved into the leftover gravy. I looked around at the teeming auditorium, guessing there had to be at least a few thousand men caged with me. I had no idea such places existed, nor should they, in a functioning society.

The men began to amuse themselves now that they were done with eating; some played cards, while others exercised. There were no weights or equipment in sight, but many of the men did push-ups or took turns using the supporting framework of the ramps to do chin-ups.

All ignored me.

I returned the tray and limped around the perimeter of the auditorium in search of a toilet. There were none that I could see, nor had there been facilities in the cell I had woken in.

I began to fear I would have to squat in a corner, and I picked up my pace around the perimeter in search of a bathroom. A loud siren echoed throughout the vast hall as I neared the end of my circuit. I followed the gazes of the men to a screen above the canteen displaying a sequence of numbers in which I could discern no meaning; but which had a profound impact on the those around me. Some rose and began moving off in seemingly random groups, pushing past me as they headed towards one wall or another around the square. Four doors had opened along opposite walls; a letter displayed above each. The men started moving through in an orderly fashion, disappearing within.

I joined one of the queues and shuffled through the doorway. A flash of red and a brief siren. Rough hands flung me away; men swore at my stupidity. I stumbled from the queue, my injured knee nearly collapsing under me. One of the men at the back of the line showed me the tattoo on the inside of his wrist, before shaking his head and turning away.

A glance at my own wrist, and everything came together neatly. On the inside of my arm, still raised and red, lay a black tattoo — a sequence of numbers, with a bar code above them. It was not yet my turn to use the restroom. Eventually my numbers were displayed and, at last, I had the chance to relieve myself.

Soon after, another siren sounded. Prisoner bar codes and cell numbers moved down the screen, sending men off to their allotted cells in an orderly fashion. It was as I shuffled to my cell I realised I had seen no guards or prison staff. The little omnipresent red lights ran the prison with complete efficiency. The feeding and toilet ritual was repeated again many hours later, though this time the toilets were first. I found I mastered the system quickly. Everything was random; no discernable patterns, no set routine, no cell to call home.

That night, as I lay on the hard mattress of a different, but identical cell, my only thoughts were of Anna. Weakness overcame me, and I wept at what had befallen my beautiful wife; my one true friend and the love of my life.

4.

The next day came, or what I assumed to be another day. No one had come to check my wounds or my condition, so I took it upon myself to undo the bandages. My left hand was blue and swollen, the knuckles gashed and torn. An attempt to move my index finger had me swearing and catching my breath. My knee was less injured, and I decided to leave the bandage off. I was halfway through re-wrapping my hand when the door opened with a flash of red from above. I rushed to finish and be out the door, reluctant to again feel the punishment meted out for tardiness.

Twenty minutes later I sat finishing another tasteless meal in the overcrowded auditorium. The food was the same as the day before, as it probably would be the next day, and the one after that.

I looked at the hundreds of men eating around me and wondered how they came to be in such a place. Many had the look of hardened criminals, but often I came across those who seemed as out of place as I no doubt did.

It was as I sat scanning the milling crowd that I locked eyes with the tattooed man who had pulled me from my cell the day before. He sat some twenty meters to my right, his back to the table, eyes upon me. He left the game of cards to approach me, his pack, all of them covered in the same tattoos and scars, didn't notice his departure.

I feigned indifference and tried to ignore the wave of anxiety churning my stomach as I watched him approach. That he was a member of one of the gangs that ruled the slums was without question, his confidence supreme as the crowd parted to allow him through.

He sat opposite me and stared with dark eyes that gave no hint to his intentions. The tattoos on his face were indecipherable, many stood on raised ridges of skin that looked to have been cut at different times, and with different implements. I had seen enough documentaries to recognize that the artistically drawn numbers and symbols had great significance to those like him, and the raised scars that crisscrossed his face and arms represented various milestones in his criminal career. I stared back and showed nothing of my fear.

When he spoke his lightly accented voice was soft, in contrast to his fearsome appearance.

"I heard you yelling when you did that," he nodded to my injured hand. "I was all fucked up when I got here as well."

I shook my head slightly, not knowing what to say; the sound of someone speaking to me was strangely unnerving.

"You know they would have kept going till they killed you? In the cell. They can do whatever they want here, it's not like a normal pen. They killed one guy a few months back. Hit his head on the first zap and he was done, fuckers kept going till he was cooked."

He looked away from me, back to the group of scarred veterans; the card game had ceased and all were watching us. One of them stood and flashed a hand signal too fast for me to follow. The young man sitting opposite glanced at me as he rose; concern visible even under the black numbers and symbols marring his face.

"I'm Riley," I blurted.

He didn't reply at first. then "Mateo," and was gone. He endured a brief reprimand on his return, which he shrugged off, picking up his cards and bidding the others do likewise. A few hostile looks were thrown my way then the game was joined.

A moment later my number came up and the strange meeting was forgotten as I lined up to use the toilets, shuffling along with the rest of the cattle, my eyes glazed and head hung. As I came back out another siren blared and the screen showed a single sequence of numbers, and the letter Q. There was a stir among the milling men; those new to the prison checked their numbers, as did I; the number was mine. The door marked Q was easy to find: I simply followed the expectant looks of the other men. I walked quickly through the crowd of curious onlookers, my eyes avoiding theirs. I was the chosen one; and my apprehension grew as I left the hushed auditorium and walked alone down the metal corridor to my mysterious summons.

• • •

The steel passageway ran straight and unerring, the silence oppressive once the doors slid shut behind me. The doors at the far end opened into a small square room, lit by a harsh white light emanating from the walls themselves and unadorned, save for a red line dividing the floor in two. I stepped in and peered about, jumping slightly when the doors slid shut behind me.

And then … nothing. Nothing but the sound of my breath in the silence. I stood, staring blankly ahead at the glaring white walls, defeated and with little care for what might come.

Time dragged on. My knee began to throb, my thoughts to wander.

"It doesn't paint itself, you know."

"You sure? It's pretty white," I muttered without turning.

Anna sighed and put down the tape she was using to edge the living room wall.

"I told you, it's supposed to be, it makes the room seem bigger because it reflects light, remember?"

I stood looking at the half painted wall for a few moments, long enough for Anna to see a need to reinforce her argument.

"You remember how bad Ben's place looked before? I did the colors for that and you don't hear him complaining."

"Well that's because you're his boss," I mused, brushing a stray hair back from her face. The drop of white paint on the end of her nose continued to dry.

"I'm always the boss when it comes to design, pumpkin. You just leave the thinking to me" she said with a grin.

I dropped the roller into the tray and ruffled the drop sheets with my feet "Ever wanted to do it with a filthy, sexy painter?" I murmured, my eyes hooding over.

"Yep, with a sexy one that is. You just get back to work."
She strutted back to the ladder and picked up the roll of tape,
pretending not to notice me as I stalked towards her.

A green light flashed opposite, and a moment later a panel opened at head height in the wall, revealing a large plasma screen. On it was the thin, bearded face of Andrew, my mother's long-time friend and reluctant family lawyer.

He peered into the screen and adjusted his glasses, as he always did when uncomfortable with a situation. I hadn't seen him in over two years; he had aged, though by the look on his face I could tell that of the two of us, I had been the most ravaged.

I stepped forward out of instinct, to be pulled up short as I crossed the red line. The room flashed scarlet and a siren wailed, freezing me with one foot in the air. I stepped back, cursing myself for being so easily controlled.

Andrews's world-weary voice echoed around me from speakers set in the walls. "Riley, I'm so sorry. I found you as soon as I could. We'll get you out, don't worry."

"Where's Anna? Have you got her back?" I asked, panic near choking me.

He avoided my eyes and ran a trembling hand though his graying hair, "Riley, there's nothing we can do. I'm so sorry."

"What the fuck do you mean there's nothing you can do? It's Anna!" I roared

He held up a hand and spoke as if I were some frightened animal. "Your whole family's here Riley. Everyone's here for you, ok? I know you feel alone in there, but you're not."

I turned away, jaw tight.

"Riley, you've been put in the wrong prison; this place was built a few years ago for convicted violators of the Steadfast Act. I can get you out on a technicality. The Intervention Officers who came to your apartment were put on suspension for misconduct the day after they arrested you. Someone was killed in an intervention and all three of them were taking four times the legal limit of stimulants. All of their interventions in the past month are under review and I've made enough noise for them to agree to let you out. You shouldn't be here at all. They just put people here because they can skip giving them access to legal advice. Your mom's come up with enough money for bail, so I can get you out … "

My voice exploded across the room, and in my anger I came close to stepping over the line again. "I don't give a fuck about me! You get her back. Don't you talk to me like she's gone; she's out there right now. You get her back. Sell everything I have, leave me in here if you have to, just find her and get her back!"

He hung his head, defeated and shamed; something I had never seen him do.

I stood silent for a moment, and struggled to regained some control. "Andrew, just leave me here, it's fine. Tell them all not to worry, just tell me you'll find her."

Even as I spoke he was shaking his head, his eyes pleading for me to stop, which I did not. "You can't tell me everyone's ready to just let her go as if she's dea … " My voice caught, and I looked away again.

"Riley, I've spent the past week doing everything I can. If I push any more they'll arrest me. I've had to keep your brothers from doing something stupid as well. You're lucky I managed to get here at all. No one's just letting her go.

You have to believe me when I tell you that if there was anything I could do, I'd be doing it. After what happened …"

I shook my head, chasing away memories of the disaster that had shaken the country to its knees and threatened to topple the government five years ago. Hundreds of videos and images had made it out of the epicenter before the army had sealed it off. Many still refused to believe that a drug could have caused such devastation, that a drug could do that to people, could destroy someone so quickly. I shook the images of emaciated corpses lying in the streets from my mind.

Not Anna, never her.

"This is bullshit, Andrew! You know Anna, and you know she would never use that shit. Why the hell would she? Why would anyone take something that would do that to you? And how would she get it, anyway?"

He stared back at me, a faraway, haunted look in his eyes. "Riley, they showed me a video. It was Anna, after they arrested her. I'm sorry, but she's gone, there's nothing anyone can do for her now."

"You saw her? Where was she? I want to see the video right now!"

He shook his head "Even if I could get a copy, which I can't, I would never show you."

"You think they couldn't fake something like that? I don't believe it, neither should any of you. For Christ's sake, it's Anna!"

He adjusted his glasses again, taking a breath and nodding. "Riley, I'm sorry, but we only have a few more minutes. I'm here to get you out, nothing more."

Silence filled the room, I stood, a shell, uncaring and ruined.

Andrew cleared his throat and sat a little straighter, his tone that of the professional lawyer again. "You'll need to sign a statement to be released. It's important that you come to terms with what's happened, if not for yourself then for your mother. You have no idea what this has done to her Riley, you know Anna was like a daughter to her."

I nodded and fought off tears.

"I'm truly sorry for what's happened Riley; I'm only trying to help you, ok? I can get everything organized by mid-morning tomorrow, if all goes well I'll get you out by midday."

Our meeting was ended by a siren and flash of red, and I left while he was still speaking. I walked numbly to my allotted cell; sitting on the thin mattress and staring into space. I was in the same position when the doors opened in the morning.

. . .

There was no choice but to file to the auditorium for the morning meal with the rest of the broken. It was obvious that my mysterious summons the previous day had aroused curiosity. I was followed by murmurs and covert stares as I collected my morning mush; it was a relief to find an unoccupied table in a corner. I sat with my back to the milling mass of men, the stupidest thing you could probably do in a prison, and stared vacantly at the lukewarm bowl of gruel in front of me.

"What was that about yesterday?"

I jerked upright at hearing a voice so close. Mateo sat next to me, his back to the table. It took me a moment to realize what he was talking about.

"Nothing. A lawyer."

His eyes widened, tattoos writhing. "They letting you out?"

I shrugged and looked back to my untouched meal, screaming in my mind for him to leave me be, that whatever he wanted would not come.

He shuffled closer. "I've been in here two years and never seen no fucking lawyer. You rich?"

I ignored him.

"Are you sending her stuff?" he asked casually, though the way he lowered his voice was not missed.

I spun to face him, my eyes wide and questioning.

"Just saying that I've heard if you've got the cash you can send them stuff, you know, like food and shit, make sure they get their share."

"How do you know about her?"

"Fuck everyone knows. Remember when you got here? You were all fucked up. The walls are thick but the doors let some noise out. We could hear you."

I could remember little of my first night, though my swollen left hand and throbbing knee were constant reminders of my assault on the door.

"What do you mean send her stuff? My wife is in the Exclusion Zone … she took … they said she took it." My heart began beating wildly, adrenalin pumping.

He leaned in closer, his breath on my face. "I've heard of people," he glanced around with suspicious eyes "they'll get things in there for you. It's pretty bad you know. Not much food or medicine or shit like that, they're just dumping them all in there to die now, hardly any supply drops. Maybe I can set it up, for a fee and a lawyer to get me the fuck out of here." He leaned away, gauging my reaction.

The noise of the prison faded away, as did Mateo's voice as he leaned in again to clarify his proposition. My mind raced, a near infinite jigsaw puzzle of actions and possibilities, of hopes and logistics swirled through my mind, locking together in perfection, my path clear. I had only felt such clarity of purpose once in my life; the moment I saw Anna struggling along the teeming sidewalk with a blank art canvass and asked her to share a cab, then soon after, my life.

I leapt to my feet and grabbed him by the shirt, dragging his face to within inches of mine. My rapid change was a shock for him, he leaned away and dared not meet my gaze as I whispered my request.

He looked at me as if I'd gone mad, "That's not what I said. I can't organize that. There's no point anyway, you can't stop it." he protested.

He struggled to push me away.

"You'll do it for two hundred and fifty thousand, cash."

"You're fucked in the head," he said, squirming from my grasp and turning to leave.

I spun him to face me, and doubled my offer to five hundred thousand. It was everything I had in the world, and more. He met my gaze and said nothing for a moment, before nodding slowly and waving away the tattooed men who came sprinting to his aid. We sat together and spoke privately for the next hour until the siren called us back to our cells.

. . .

I paced my cell for the next four hours, mumbling like a lunatic, fists balled, breath hissing through clenched teeth. When the doors opened I was the first to reach the auditorium, rushing to stand in front of the screen, my body trembling. I glanced at Mateo as he entered with his ink-scarred group. They watched me and muttered amongst themselves as they sat.

Time dragged by, the minutes impossibly long as I looked from the closed doors to the screen and back, willing my summons to appear, mumbling through clenched teeth, "Jesus, come on Andrew, come on, come on."

Nothing happened.

The men began to eat and still I stood, my eyes never leaving the screen. Soon the toilet ritual began, I ignored my chance to go. I don't know how long I stood there being jostled by the other prisoners — long enough for men to look at me as if my mind had gone.

When my number finally came up and the doors opened I was through them and pounding down the corridor as fast as my injured knee would allow. The doors at the far end took an eternity to open, and I spilled through them as they were still sliding apart, hoping to find Andrew on the screen opposite.

He wasn't there, and I was forced to wait a lifetime for him to appear. When his gray face materialized he looked startled by my appearance. I stepped over the line and ignored the siren and flash of red, my face inches from his.

"Get me out of here, Andrew. Now."

5.

"*Come on, it was funny, I heard you laughing.*"

Anna rolled her eyes. "*I laughed once, even that was generous. I hate that slapstick crap. I knew it was going to be like that.*"

I turned to her, the lights of passing cars flashed across her face as she weaved our small hybrid through the late night traffic.

"*You're telling me you don't find an alien getting hit in the groin hilarious? Its comic genius! And who would have thought a woman's top would rip off so easily, and at such an inappropriate time, amazing!*"

I was full of popcorn, and hyped up on sugar and caffeine.

"*Oh my god,*" eyes rolled again

"*Good thing it only went for two and a half hours. I'm telling Ben to go see it.*"

"*Don't! He hardly ever goes, don't make him waste his yearly cinema outing on a break dancing extra-terrestrial.*"

"*I will. We'll talk about it for months, it'll be great.*"

My foot was on the dash, I was reveling in my childish belligerence.

"I'm warning him," Anna mumbled.

"I warning you," I gently tugged at a strand of her hair, my eyes slits.

I was pushed back in the seat as we put on a burst of speed. Anna cut into the traffic streaming across the bridge, the city center gaudy and sprawling behind us as we climbed the long steady arch.

"I think my little boy's had too much sugar, hasn't he?" she snickered.

"Not enough, you wait until I get you home! I might even trip and accidentally rip your top off."

"Oh god."

The river passed underneath, wide and black. To our right and ahead the city stretched from horizon to horizon, the only break in the sea of light a large blacked-out quarter on the left, as if the river had flooded a part of the city.

I looked away and saw Anna do the same, an awkward silence taking hold. The road veered away from the Exclusion Zone, and it was soon forgotten.

"Riley this is futile! You need to get back in the car right now before they see us. I cant save you a second time."

I ignored Andrews's warning and left him in the idling car, walking towards coils of razor wire stretching into the night on either side. In the distance, through two abandoned city blocks, stood the well-guarded and starkly illuminated walls of the Exclusion Zone. The chain-link fencing of the original emergency barricade had long since gone, replaced by a towering wall of cement with guard towers and sweeping lights keeping vigil on both sides of the thirty-foot high barrier. This is where it had begun, ground zero, oblivion for thousands.

The freeway buzzed with evening traffic barely five hundred meters behind me, the commuters snug in their apathy. None would give the abandoned area more than a passing thought as they crossed the river into the city center; the Zone, and all those within it, forgotten. I envied them, would have given anything for Anna and I to be part of the stream of traffic curving away into the night.

Gravel crunched underfoot as I crossed the barren expanse of asphalt and neared the razor wire. Signs warned of dire consequences should anyone attempt to cross, the penalty for such action death.

I froze as car headlights lit me up from behind.

My panic was momentary, they moved on, sweeping along the razor wire as the car turned off the road and drove past us, stopping inches from the wire fencing

The vehicle sat idling for a moment before a well-dressed women of middle age got out and placed a bunch of flowers underneath the coiled wire. She knelt a moment, speaking quietly, her words a mystery. A few moments later her shoulders began to shudder and she buried her face in her hands.

"Riley, I'm leaving right now," Andrew said, touching my shoulder. That he had left the car to get me made clear his apprehension.

"Just wait a minute," I mumbled, walking towards the kneeling women. I was close enough to hear her sobbing when she scrambled to her feet and got back into her car. I yelled for her to wait as she reversed and spun away, leaving me standing bewildered in the glow of Andrew's headlights.

"Riley, for Christ's sake lets go before you make this worse!"

A small photo was stuck amongst the flowers she had so carefully placed against the wire. I prized it from the wilting gardenias and held it up under one of the security lights. A man stood with a smiling wife and two children, his face bliss. A brief message had been written across the bottom.

To my darling husband, you will never be lost to us. Your loving wife.

I looked from the photo to the road behind me. The lights of her vehicle merged with the traffic and she was quickly gone, lost amongst the endless flow of cars crossing the river into the city center. I looked back to the photo for a few moments, struggling to make sense of why a man like that would leave a wife and children alone in the world. I put it back amongst the flowers with great care, my stomach knotted at the thought of what his family must have gone through.

A second later such thoughts were forgotten, as lights of a vehicle flicked on and came racing towards us from the base of the distant barricade.

Andrew barely waited for me to close the door.

The tires screeched and we raced across the expanse of bitumen. I turned and watched the military vehicle stop on the other side of the fence and discharge three soldiers, one of whom reached through and snatched the flowers from the amongst the wire.

"Why the hell did I let you talk me into that? We could have been arrested! We probably will be! You need to be careful, Riley, I wont be there to help you again … are you listening to me Riley?"

I lent back and watched the city race by in a blur of neon, ignoring Andrew's fretting as I thought of the woman, and the man who had been her husband. Why someone who appeared so normal and happy would take it and doom himself was beyond reason. Though I supposed drug addicts had little time for reason.

Soon after I resolved to forget the troubles of others; as the world had forgotten Anna and I.

• • •

We didn't speak for the remainder of the trip. As we pulled up in front of my building forty minutes later, Andrew broke the silence enveloping us.

"Please Riley, let me drive you to your mothers. I told her I'd take you straight there. I can't show up without you."

I looked out the window to the quiet street, and the park opposite, illuminated here and there by soft yellow lights. The exorbitant rates we had to pay to keep the gardens green were worth it; Anna and I spent many summer nights walking through the glades, lost in the soft netherworld.

"No, I can't face my family yet. I need some time," I said, my eyes and mind far away.

He sighed disapprovingly and swore under his breath.

I spoke before he had a chance to start, "You're clear on what needs to be done with the business, and Mateo?"

He took off his glasses and made a show of massaging his temple before he nodded.

"Good, I'll call you tomorrow at 10."

He nodded again and I opened the door. "This is between us, Andrew. My family can't know. I have your word?"

He put his glasses back on and scowled, "Riley you already made me swear. I won't tell them, but you need to listen to me — there's nothing you can do to bring her back. I'm sorry to be the one to say it, but you need to hear it. You need to accept what is and treasure the people you still have in your life. Don't do anything to make things worse for yourself."

"I'll call you tomorrow," I closed the door and waved for him to go.

He waited before leaving, obviously contemplating his chances of changing my mind. A moment later he shook his head and pulled away from the curb, the hum of his car fading away into the night.

I stood in the quiet street, listening to the distant drone of the city, punctuated now and then by sirens and the faint thump of police helicopters; the world we had so recently been a part of now hostile and alien.

The burden of what I'd set in motion began to weigh heavily on me. I began to feel doubt, to see how precarious my plan was, how the slightest misstep would see me tumbling into an abyss, never to see my Anna again.

I shook my head and took a step towards the stairs to our apartment in an effort to stem the tide of hopelessness that threatened to engulf me — I struggled, and failed to take another.

Move man, you have to move.

But I could not, fear and doubt continued to worm away at me. I was alone in the world, my plan nothing but a fool's desperation. I broke out in a cold sweat, the world began to spin — and then the trees in the park across the road stirred in the wind, a warm breeze whispered through their leaves and flowed over me. I turned to face it and closed my eyes, breathing deep, the air heavy with the scent of jasmine.

The hope I was desperately in need of began to well inside me, and by the time the breeze died away I was myself again.

I bolted up the stairs to the apartment, knowing I would have little time before my family descended on me. They would ignore my pleas for solitude and would soon arrive to console me, something I had little time for; I had to be quick if I was to dodge them.

The lights flicked on automatically when I opened the door. I nearly buckled under the weight of memory. We were snuggled on the couch, watching movies while she absentmindedly stroked my arm. I was teasing her as she botched her turn at cooking. She stood with lips pursed and hands on hips, contemplating the position of a table as a general would his artillery, while I stood ready to drag.

She was everywhere and nowhere, our home a shell without her.

I moved quickly, only pausing for the briefest moment when I came across her scarf by the couch; I allowed myself a few seconds of bliss as I held it to my face. Deep breaths filled my lungs with her scent, my ears with her laughter. She was with me and then gone, fading away to leave me standing alone in the living room, my face buried in the soft folds of material.

. . .

I made it out of the apartment with little time to spare. The shadows in the park concealed me moments before a car pulled up outside our building. My mother and two brothers tore up the stairs. A few seconds later the apartment lit up as they went from room to room searching for me. I turned and hurried through the park, sending a brief message to my older brother that I was fine, that I would call them tomorrow. I then blocked all calls and messages; the only number in my contacts I left open was Andrew's.

I reached the warehouse in less than fifteen minutes; Anna and I had been lucky to find an apartment so close to work, though we rarely walked. There were always too many things to do on the way, life leaving little time for living.

I pulled up short when I saw the lights still on in the two-story building. It was Thursday night and long after closing time, and I swore when I saw Ben's old Ford parked outside. I cursed his diligence as I stood in the shadow of large oak and mulled over my options. There was no question that I needed to use my office tonight. I needed to access the Net and I needed more than the half hour slots set for private use.

"Jesus Ben, go home, just go home," I whispered, though I knew he wouldn't. The latest shipment would have arrived, he would not leave until everything was checked and ready for distribution, the task likely to take the remainder of the night.

I took a deep breath and stepped from the shadows, striding across the road and preparing myself for the outpouring of grief he would no doubt unleash on me. The security lights flicked on as I neared the front entrance. I punched in the access code and rushed inside; fears that my family would come racing around the corner hounded me.

Ben's heavy footsteps pounded across the warehouse floor as I entered the small reception area. For a brief moment I eyed the stairs to my office, coveting the seclusion they promised, until Ben came thumping down the hallway and threw himself at me, encompassing me in a crushing hug as he wept.

Ben was a large man, over six feet tall, with a thick build made strong by years working as a laborer and tree arborist; there was little I could do but endure his sobbing embrace, though for me grief was now an obstacle to avoid when possible, to overcome when not. I returned his hug with dry eyes and clear purpose.

"Jesus Riley —I tried, we all did. Cops dragged me out of the station and told me if I pushed it again I'd be sent to prison for three months. I'm sorry, I didn't know what else to do."

We moved into the warehouse proper, two thousand square meters, most of it taken up by stacks of crates just in, and others ready to leave. I led Ben under the stairs of the half loft and sat him at the table, filling a glass of water and pushing it across to him as I sat opposite.

"Ben I know you did everything you could, I know you. I don't want you to contact the police again or push for information on Anna in anyway. There's nothing you or they can do."

My voice, devoid of emotion, seemed to shock him.

"Ben, I need you to do something for me."

He took a few more deep breaths and a sip of water to settle himself, his weathered face still wet with tears

"My family will be here any moment looking for me. I need you to tell them you haven't seen me, will you do that for me?"

Confusion wrinkled his sun-hardened face. He opened his mouth to speak, but I cut him off.

"Please don't ask why. Everything's fine, I just need some time. I'll see them soon, just not now, promise me you'll do it."

He thought deeply for a moment, as he did on all matters of import. Ben was honest to a fault and completely without guile; a quality Anna and I loved, but others mistakenly took for a sign of a simple mind. Though slow to make a decision, once it was made there could be no turning him, he would follow through with a ponderous determination few possessed. When he finally nodded with a long exhalation I knew without a doubt his collaboration was assured. I left him sitting at the small lunch table and hid at the back of the warehouse, behind a pile of unopened crates. A few minutes later a car screeched into the warehouse parking lot, two doors slamming.

Ben sat at the table, head hung. My stomach knotted at the thought of being discovered by my family and swept up in their grief. The voices of my two brothers echoed through the warehouse as soon as Ben opened the door, and I pulled back deeper into my hideaway.

Joshua, my older brother, was the first to speak as they tore into the warehouse; he sounded in a near panic. "Ben, have you seen Riley? He's not at home."

Ben's voice was steady and he spoke without pause, "I haven't seen him boys, I wish I knew where he was, I was hoping he'd show up, I'm sorry."

"Jesus where is he? What the hell does he think he's doing? You call us if you hear from him Ben, even if he says not to, ok? We'll be back at his place with mum for a while but we're not staying there. I don't want her there if the cops come for some reason. We're staying at The Maple on 46th. You know it?"

"Sure Josh."

Silence for a few moments.

"You're still ok here, right?" Josh asked.

"Yes, its fine … I'm fine, I work better by myself."

More silence.

"Ben … "

"Josh, I looked through her office, it's bullshit, all of it. You know Anna, there's no way she would. Jesus, both of you've known her for twice as long I have."

"I know … but … "

"But what? Come on boys, why the hell would she? I don't believe it for a second and neither should you," Ben's voice was beginning to waver, "It's a mistake, or a set up or something, I don't know. She wouldn't touch that shit."

Ethan spoke next, and when he did it was all I could do to not rage from my hiding place. "Josh it doesn't matter now. Anna's gone, she's not coming back. We need to find Riley and get back to mum."

"You call us Ben, no matter what."

They left moments later, the car screeching away into the night. They would likely continue searching the streets for me for some time.

I emerged from my hiding place and watched as Ben walked back to a half unpacked crate and stood motionless, staring vacantly ahead. Lying did not come easily to him, especially to my brothers. I suddenly realized that what I was about to tell him would be devastating. Anna and I, and this warehouse, were all he had.

He turned as I approached, his face red with pent up emotion.

"What about your mum, Riley? You know she hasn't slept since she found out. You need to go home."

He looked drained; dark circles ringed his eyes, his thinning, sandy-blonde hair was unwashed and disheveled.

"Ben, sit down, please. I need to talk to you."

I led him back to the table and sat with him again, this time taking a drink of water myself.

"I'm sorry you had to do that, but I can't face them right now. I'll see them tomorrow. I have something to tell you, but before I do I want you to know that I wouldn't be doing this unless I had to."

He scowled slightly, but to his credit nodded for me to continue.

"I'm selling the business. I'm hoping it'll be done within a few days."

He leapt to his feet, eyes wide, "What! I can run it for you Riley, as long as you need. You don't need to sell, you think Anna would want you to just throw all of her work away?"

I held a hand up to calm him. "Ben, please just listen. This is something I need to do. I'm giving you some of the money from the sale, you'll be looked after."

"Riley, everything's running fine. Take as much time off as you need, take a year off. I'll manage everything. The shipment's checked off, it's being picked up tomorrow. All of it's sold, and half the next one."

I rose from the table. "Ben I have to, please understand I wouldn't be doing it if there was any other way."

"Any other way for what Riley? What are you doing? And who's buying it?"

"A Jian Imports, I'm taking them up on the offer they made a few months ago."

Ben's eyes widened, his face flashing red and contorting, "Fucking them! You know they were at that party we all went to the night before she went missing; they probably did this to her. They could have spiked her drink or something. I've been thinking about it, it all makes sense, they're trying to get rid of us. I'll fucking kill them before they set foot in here."

He paced back and forth in a fury; anger was something I had never seen in Ben, I was shocked to silence.

"We built this place. You, me and Anna. We cant just hand it over, not after what's happened."

I regretted the next words I spoke as soon as they left me. He halted his tirade instantly, stopping as if he'd run into a wall.

"What?" he gasped, his voice barely audible.

I laid my entire plan out to him, barely pausing for breath, going over all that needed to be done in the next few days, the burden lighter once shared.

He stood unmoving as I spoke, the color draining from his face. Silence filled the warehouse as the magnitude of what I'd told him sunk in.

He hung his head for a moment, nodding slightly with jaw set. When he raised his eyes and met mine they burned with purpose.

"I'm coming with you."

6.

I left Ben in the warehouse, taking the stairs two at a time to my office above.

The lights flicked on as I entered and mumbled the password to power up my work station. A small beep rang through the room and I returned to the door. I put my finger in the small scanner and spoke the name of our long dead cat slowly and clearly.

"Dumpling."

A reassuring tone sounded and the room filled with the hum of three computers, printers and countless other gadgets powering up. I swept the piles of papers, pens and fast food wrappers from my desk and repeated a similar procedure to log into my computer.

A quick retinal scan and I was online.

Uploading the hundreds of pictures I had taken in our apartment, and then matching them with the correct descriptions, took hours. I swore bitterly every thirty minutes when I had to submit to another scan to stay online. Though the need to limit people's use of computers was obvious, the health and social problems caused by overuse being impossible to ignore, the few seconds it took to be back online infuriated me, as it always did.

Once I had uploaded the files it took only minutes for everything Anna and I owned to be matched up with buyers around the country; the furniture we had collected over the years, her clothes and the jewelry her grandmother had left her, our car and bikes. Everything sold in moments. Prices were automatically haggled by the system according to the user's set limits and in seconds it was all gone; the life and home we had built together now nothing more than digits on a screen.

I selected the company's express service; I would have the money in three days. I re-scanned my eye at the computer's request, buying another thirty minutes before I stood to stretch my aching back.

Anna's desk stood opposite mine, on the other side of the room; ordered and neat, as it always was.

"It's going to bust! You never learn do you?" I warned.

Anna continued her assault on the pen in her mouth, eyes never leaving the computer screen.

I put her coffee on the desk and peeked at her work.

"I told you I can't have coffee, the diet, remember? And you're over the line Mr." she warned, sipping her coffee regardless and glancing down at the imaginary border separating our work spaces. Anna seemed to have no problem keeping to her side. I, on the other hand, launched countless incursion, in defiance to the new work rule both of us had agreed on.

I wandered to the window and leaned on the frame, gulping down my de'café; Anna, Ben and Lucy, our secretary, had banned me from real coffee, the intervention coming after an epic binge that left an entire month's invoices in a shambles.

"So we're definitely going- right? No backing out this time?" I asked, watching as she typed code with one hand and gulped coffee with the other.

Anna sighed and continued her assault on the keyboard "Not if I haven't finished this."

I pushed myself off the window frame. "Not this time lady! We're going, we need to."

She put the coffee down and popped the pen back in her mouth, mumbling around the twisted plastic, "Hey, I want to alright, but this needs to be done, and you hassling me isn't helping."

"Oh, you want to go now! But just cant get away from work huh? Nice try lady. It's a free bar you know, I'll get you as many Mojitos as you like. I'll be your little party assistant."

She swivelled her chair to face me, a grin taking shape, "As many as I like? Look at you big spender! So you'll get me as many of the free drinks as I like, huh?"

"Yep. Sometimes I like to treat my bitches you know. We'll roll there in my rig, you can get wasted." I grinned, draining my cup and throwing it to the bin beside my desk.

An eyebrow raised at that, "I'm not drinking for a few months, remember?"

I shrugged and picked up my cup up from the floor next to the bin - I always missed. "Boring! Come on, you can have a few."

She went back to typing, shaking her head.

"Well then, I shall shower you in the finest soft drinks available my dear, I'll spare no expense."

An eyebrow raised again, a smile creeping onto her face as she rolled her chair towards me and hugged me around the waist, pressing her head to my stomach.

"What a man I have."

I looked away from her desk, lest memory break me, and wandered to the window. The coming day was a streak of gray on the horizon. I was tired, so exhausted I had trouble seeing clearly; my strained eyes and slow thought process reminding me of the sense in the government's crackdown on excessive computer use.

I stepped closer to the window and looked down at the empty street, resting my forehead against the cold glass with my eyes closed, her scarf in my hands "I'm coming babe. I'm coming,"

Ben's voice startled me, I spun to see him shuffling in the doorway, a ledger held before him.

"What?" I mumbled, blinking my eyes to focus.

"I said you need to sign off on the inventory."

He took a step forward and cleared his throat "Maybe you should have a break, when's the last time you slept?"

"Give it to me", I mumbled, stuffing the scarf in my pocket and signing the ledger without looking.

Ben looked at my chaotic scrawl, then back to me "I'm done with most of it. I can get it all finished by this afternoon, but we'll need the accounts and bank records reconciled."

I nodded and stepped back to my desk, staring vacantly at the identity request on the screen, my mind far from accounts and bank records.

"Ben I need to talk to you about what I'm going to do. You need to listen and think hard before you answer. You understand there's nothing I won't do to get her back? You realize that don't you?"

The room was silent for a time, and when I looked up from the computer and into Ben's eyes they were steady, his resolve firm.

"I'm with you till the end, Riley."

. . .

The predawn air was cold, my arms crossed as I walked through the park. My mind was filled with dollar amounts, times and people; a jigsaw puzzle of near insurmountable logistics. I gave little thought to what might happen if I succeeded, and none to failure.

The world brightened around me and I picked up my pace, cutting across the grass and through stands of trees like some thief in the night. The park ended at the sidewalk opposite the apartment and I bolted across and up the stairs, desperate to avoid any neighbors who might be early risers.

I flicked on the lights and stumbled to the kitchen, not bothering to fill the kettle, instead mixing four heaped spoons of ground coffee into a glass of water from the tap.

I gagged as I swallowed the bitter pulp.

"Jesus, I need something stronger," I hissed, moving into the living room, rubbing my face and stretching my eyes. A host of vicious sounding drugs flashed through my mind, the military's never ending quest for efficiency enhancement leaving a plethora of past favorites available to the public.

I mumbled something about going to a pharmacy and sat on the couch, resting my eyes for a moment.

7.

My phone ripped me from sleep.

I stumbled forward, mashing my fingers into the keys to answer the call and hanging up instead. Bright sunlight streamed in through the kitchen window and I was appalled when I saw the time — 10:30am.

I called Andrew back immediately while I paced back and forth, fuming at such a lapse and willing my mind to clear.

Andrews's drawn face filled the screen, "Riley, where the hell have you been?"

He peered at me, adjusting his glasses "Are you ok? Jesus where are you? I'm sending your brothers, you look near dead."

I blinked and shook my head; his face remained blurred, "I told you what I need you to do and that's all Andrew, I'm fine. Is it done?"

He shook his head and looked away before sighing, "He should be out in two days, once we post bail and pay various other fees. Riley — I checked him out, I don't understand what you're doing with someone like that, those gangs are out of control."

"I don't fucking care what he's done, Andrew! I need him out!"

His face reddened, and the glasses came off, "You listen to me Riley and you listen well; I'm not sure what you're planning, but its obviously something that's going to cause your family more pain. I want you to go and see your mother right now. If you don't then you can forget about me helping you. Do you understand?"

I stammered as I sought a response; his tirade cut short my flimsy rebuke.

"Riley, are you listening to what I'm saying? Unless see your family right now you can forget about all of it. What's happened to you and your wife is beyond terrible, but you're not the only one. You can't go on treating your mother like this, she's about to fall to pieces and your brothers aren't faring much better."

I surrendered under the relentless barrage, a hand over my eyes. "Ok, ok, stop. I'll call her. Just tell me you've progressed with the business."

His sighed and made a show of massaging his temple, before putting his glasses back on.

"I've contacted A Jian with your offer and they seem willing. I'll talk to them again after you've seen your mother."

He softened his voice somewhat, content with his victory.

"We can discuss it further when I've heard from her. Oh, and clean yourself up a little Riley, you know what your mother will be like if she sees you like that, have a shave at least."

The screen flickered and he was gone.

I threw the phone on the couch and stalked back and forth, running a hand through greasy hair and breathing deeply.

After a few minutes of searching for a way out of the inevitable, and finding none, I sat on the couch and took a deep breath to steady myself. That which I'd been so desperate to avoid now seemed inescapable, and I prepared myself for the outpouring of grief that would come from my family.

Moments later I picked up the phone and called my mother.

• • •

They knocked on the door twenty minutes later. Their arrival came sooner than I expected, I'd had little time to prepare myself for the deluge of despair that descended with them.

My mother threw herself at me when I opened the door, hugging me with a strength that bellied her frail build and flooding me with a barrage of soothing, nonsensical babble. Colorful bangles rattled up and down her forearms as she stroked my face and fussed over me.

My two brothers joined our tearful embrace in the doorway, I led the sobbing pack inside and succumbed to my mothers manic doting while my brothers vented.

"We won't let this go Riley, no way. They won't get away with this bullshit," Ethan raved as he stalked back and forth, muscled shoulders straining against his thin t-shirt. His eyes were red and swollen, his voice wavering.

"No fucking way," Joshua promised.

My mother wiped her eyes, bangles jingling, "I'll organize the service, bub. We can do it in the park, remember how much she loved the glade under the oak? I've still got that photo you sent me. She looked so happy. You two were always going there."

"We'll organize it all, don't worry about any of it," Josh promised, "I filled out the forms they left, you just need to sign. It needs to be done Riley, the initial therapy session is mandatory. We'll just get it over with, if we don't the police will drag you there. I called, they can see you tomorrow morning."

"I'll come with you," my mother promised.

"We're all here for you, Riley."

They spoke, and I listened to none of it.

· · ·

"Come in Riley, take a seat."

The woman ushered me into her office, placing a folder on the table as she sat. She waved to the chair opposite and started flicking through the folder. The room was small, cramped even; I guessed fitting a hundred or so of them in the squat, fort-like building would necessitate that.

She was perhaps a few years younger than I, no more than late twenties; her hair in a matronly bun, glasses small and stylish. She, like the room, was unremarkable and unmemorable, as was the security officer standing behind me.

She spent a few minutes going over some papers on the desk, nodding to herself and glancing up at me now and then. I could feel, rather than see, cameras dissecting me.

"It says here there was an incident during your intervention. Are you ok?"

"Yes, I'm fine." I shifted in my chair at the memory of throttling orange hair. She gave me a quick up and down.

"It's natural to be angry when something like this happens to us, Riley. Incidents like this are exactly why interventions are being phased out, it's barbaric. I'm sorry you had to go through that."

She lent back slightly, her face assuming a mask of concern. Everything about her seemed contrived.

"And what about now, how do you feel now? Do you still feel anger towards others?"

"No."

"And what about Anna?"

My jaw tightened slightly, something she didn't miss.

"What do you mean?", I asked, shifting in my chair and avoiding her eyes.

"Riley, anger is perfectly natural in a situation like this. No one would blame you for feeling anger towards your ex-wife."

I sat as if stone, biting down on the inside of my cheek hard enough to draw blood.

"Riley tell me how you feel about her. It says here you saw her taking a prohibited substance. How did that make you feel? That she would do something like that with no care for what might happen to her, or to you after she was gone."

My confused scowl sent her rifling through the papers on her desk.

"This is your signature isn't it, Riley?"

She held the form up for me to see, the signature was mine; perfect, not what I had been forced to scrawl during the intervention.

"Yes"

She put the form down, her demeanour slightly triumphant, a predator closing on her prey.

"So, tell me how it felt that she would do that."

I shifted in my seat again, the security officer standing behind me did the same. The nails of my clenched fist bit deep into my palm under the table. I couldn't speak, though she seemed not to care.

"Riley, you need to understand that Anna wasn't in control anymore. I don't want you to feel that she loved you any less for the things she might have said or done in her last few days"

I nodded and looked away.

"And there's nothing to feel guilty about Riley. It says here you reported her. You did the right thing. Right now, she is in the best place for those like her. It was a brave thing you did Riley."

I nodded again, blood trickled from the inside of my cheek. I swallowed it, the pain and taste kept me sharp, kept me from betraying myself.

"I see here that your family is with you, that's important. Let them help you through this."

"I will."

"And Anna's family?", some more shuffling through papers.

I saved her the time, "She has none, her mother died three years ago ... cancer"

"Yes I see that here, but her father? I couldn't find anything on him."

"He's in Brazil. Anna only met him once when she was twenty. Her mother went there looking for work. When her visa ran out she came back, he wouldn't" I shrugged my shoulders. "I sent him an email. He knows, but I doubt I'll hear anything from him."

She was nodding, pretending to listen while she wrote on a small ledger. She tore off the prescription and handed it to me.

"Take one of these three times a day. It will make things easier for you, for your anger. Don't worry if they make you a little drowsy or slow, just go with it and rest. There's enough for three months, and if you need more just let us know."

She nodded to the security officer and rose, offering me a card as I stood "Call this number if you want to talk again, Riley."

"I wont need to see you again."

She smiled "It wouldn't be me you'd be seeing anyway, it's best to see a different facilitator at each visit. Don't worry though, whoever it is will be completely fine, I can vouch for everyone working here. Just remember that if you do need to talk about what Anna did, it needs to be with us. I don't want you getting arrested, ok." She smiled again and patted me lightly on the shoulder as I left.

The heavy boots of the security officer followed me down the hall, we passed many more doors, all with red lights above; sessions in progress no doubt.

My family met me in the empty reception area, my mother hugged me the moment I was within reach.

"You ok?" Josh asked, resting a hand on my shoulder. He cast a hate-filled look to the security officer as he stalked away down the hall.

"Fine"

"A women come out a few minutes ago, she was crying, I thought she might collapse" Ethan said. "The security guy wouldn't let me near her"

We walked the two blocks back to the car together, all of us shielding our faces from the harsh sunlight. There were few people around, the tens of thousands of government workers living and working in the towering buildings would rarely brave the morning sun, every one of their needs met within the network of linked skyscrapers. I walked quickly, ignoring the questions of my mother and brothers as they struggled to keep up.

The prescription and card I threw in the trash.

· · ·

I hugged them all goodbye later that morning under a blazing sun. I lied and told them I would see them soon, that I would come when I had rested. I loved them dearly. My mother raised the three of us on her own, in a house no bigger than some living rooms—we were her world entire. She, and my two brothers would do anything for me, as I would for them — it was for that very reason I could never see them again.

Two removal trucks arrived soon after, and I had little time for emotional indulgence as the four men moved through our home checking off everything I had sold, then loading it into the waiting truck. There were few mistakes I had made. Perhaps a serial number misquoted, or a date of purchase mismatched with the item in question. The men were efficient, and by the end of the day I stood alone and heartbroken in the husk of our home. Everything save for

65

a small box of clothes and other personal effects was gone. Most of it would be in some strangers home within a few days. I wondered if some of the old furniture that Anna and I had so proudly collected over the years had come to us from a similarly ravaged life.

The enormity of what I had done loomed around me, and I left the apartment, memories of our life hounding me down the stairs and out onto the sidewalk. The afternoon sun lit up the park opposite, Anna and I had taken many strolls on such afternoons, she had wanted a dog, I didn't think the time was right.

My cell rang.

"Riley. How are you holding up?" Andrews bespectacled face filled the screen.

I gave a nod and false smile.

He cleared his throat and continued "Your mother just called me. I don't know how much longer she would have been able to go on without seeing you … "

I cut him off, "Is it done?"

His light-hearted demeanor faded, eyes darkened "I see. I had hoped that some time with your family would have put things into perspective."

"Andrew, I'm not changing my mind. If you cant, or wont help, then that's fine. But I need this done quickly and efficiently. Are you in or out?"

I stepped aside as a young mother led her two children past me and up the stairs. Hushed whispers and sideways glances accompanied them.

"Riley, just give it some time. Surely whatever you're planning can still be done in a few weeks. You'd certainly be able to negotiate a better price for the business if we waited."

I shook my head at his stubbornness and took a deep breath to calm myself "Andrew, I know what I'm doing. This is the last time I'll discuss this with you. If you decide you're working for me then that's it — you're my lawyer and you do what your client wants. If not, then I'll find someone else."

A few moments passed, and I held my breath, praying he wouldn't call my bluff.

He slumped in defeat and sighed "Alright, alright. Just promise me one thing; that whatever you do, you'll keep in touch with your mother. You know how important you are to her. Promise me that."

It was a promise I knew I might never keep. A lump welled in my throat and it was all I could do to nod and mumble that I would.

We spent the next twenty minutes discussing what needed to be done to secure Mateo's freedom and organizing the sale of our business. I assured him the money needed for his bail would be available by tomorrow and then left him to his task; confident that by this time tomorrow, Mateo would be a free man, and I would be beyond the point of return.

8.

I hailed one of the many cabs streaming past the north side of the park. The driver ceased his chatter after a few attempts at conversation and we crawled through the congested traffic in silence, the hum of the electric motor barely audible.

I paid little attention to the city as we drove; the beggars on the corners, the flashing advertisements and government announcements blaring from the large screens in the center, police cars racing by with sirens wailing. Around me hurried the teeming millions of a city swelled beyond capacity by refugees from the countryside in the west and the storm ravaged cities of the south. Most doubted the drought that was destroying the north and west would ever end, abandoned towns and farmlands would stay that way — the flooded southern cities beyond reclaiming.

"People need to start panicking, Jesus, something needs to happen, Sunni. People can't keep coming, we were full five years ago"

Anna was getting fired up, and so was the woman she spoke with. I remained on the sidelines with Ben, both of us shuffling nervously. We sipped our beers and looked for a way to escape the growing confrontation - people at the barbeque were beginning to glance in our direction, though the view over the city from the top of the skyscraper still drew the attentions of most.

"Come on Anna, you're overreacting, it's not that bad" Sunni replied, her tone slightly condescending.

"Not that bad! I suppose you think its ok that over eighty percent of our food is imported, that these people have lost everything. You probably think we should sell the desalination plants to the Chinese as well- why not? They built them. No need for our government to do anything for us, we can just pay the Chinese to water us as well."

"You cant blame the drought on the Chinese, Anna. We should be thankful they bailed us out" Sunni retorted, flicking her long bleach-blonde fringe to the side. I caught a glimpse of faded neon above her left eye. Whatever it had been was impossible to tell, the temporary implant dissolving quicker than it should- cheap work.

"I'm not blaming them for anything, it's us that have the problem. Look around, things are falling apart and no one is doing anything." Anna said with a sweep of her hand.

"What do mean not doing anything? No other country in the world gives its people the power we have, we chose this, we're in control."

Anna shook her head, an eyebrow raised "Oh please, you honestly think your little mandatory votes at the ATM or *online count? The government does what it wants, just like it always has."*

Sunni put her drink down on the railing and crossed her arms "Yes, I do think they count. Everyone has a say now, not just every four years when we get to pick a leader to do everything for us. This is real democracy, the people deciding."

"Come on Sunni, do you honestly think the majority voted for a second war in Iran? For Taiwan?"

"Yes I do Anna. I did."

At that I intervened, cutting between the two and handing Anna my beer.

"Hey you two it's a party huh, lighten up."

I led her away "Babe forget her, she's a moron" I whispered, steering us through the crowd.

Anna shook her head, her voice trembled with emotion, "She's everyone."

I turned away any time I saw a family out together, or a young couple walking arm in arm making their way through the thronging streets. The world went on oblivious, Anna and I crushed and unknown. By the time the cab arrived at our destination my head was hung, my eyes closed.

The driver turned and swore under his breath, probably assuming I was some drunk who would now refuse to pay. I quickly pressed my index finger into the reader on the back of his seat, then tapped my little finger next to it, paying my preset tip for cabs out of habit.

My destination was within sight. I ignored the pleas of beggars and the offers of women who sauntered about now that night had come. The double doors of the building were open, spilling white light into the street, along with the muffled popping of guns firing within the large brick-like structure. I paused, taking a few deep breaths to steady my nerves and find my focus, before mounting the stairs and entering the busy shooting gallery.

. . .

An hour later I stood across the road, waiting for Ben and running my fingers over the cold surface of the gun in my coat pocket.

The deal had been done in the alleyway behind the building. The young attendant, a boy no more than eighteen, had handed me the cloth wrapped pistol and three boxes of hollow point ammunition, his shaking hands betraying his excitement as he babbled.

"It's a Beretta Storm. 45mm, all polymer. It's hardly been shot."

I had nodded confidently and pretended I knew what he was talking about as I looked the gun over.

The boy continued to praise the weapons, "It's the one the cops and army used to use, the bullets are hollow points, highest velocity you can get. Man, they make a bang, we shot this pumpkin with one, blew it to bits, it was nuts!"

I had handed him the money and left while he was still talking.

The weight of the weapon in my pocket was comforting, the surface cool. I stood in the darkness across the road from the shooting gallery and scanned the pedestrians for any sign of Ben.

"Sorry, I can't quite remember what you two were saying"

Anna stood with the earmuffs around her neck, an eyebrow raised. The square target in her hand held the silhouette of a man, - five bullet holes in the heart, two more just grazing the right eye. The other she held was mine, the results less than impressive.

Ben and I shared a brief look, each hoping to the other might come up with a witty remark or hole-proof excuse to stave her off.

"You were saying something about women not having natural skill with guns, they can never be as good as men, something like that, right?"

She had the look of a hunter whose prey had run out of maneuvers, she was enjoying our last moments. The gallery echoed with the crack of gunfire, the air thick with the scent of burnt powder. Ben and I held our empty Glocks at our sides, Anna's sat smoking on the bench behind her.

"Don't worry boys, I'll protect you from the terrorists."

"You're a freak Anna, you shouldn't be shooting that well after just twenty minutes, you've done it before" Ben said.

I took his lead, though we both knew she hadn't, "Yeah, this is bullshit, I bet you've already been here so you could show us up."

"Oh really, and what was all that about your natural superiority? You'd think even if I had shot before, which you know I haven't, that you two would beat me anyway. You know, all that killer instinct you were bragging about."

"The guy spent more time showing you how to do it" I squeaked.

"Well maybe that's why women are better than men, we know how to listen and learn, rather than assuming we'll be the best in the world at something just because we have hairy chests."

I gave up and slunk over, putting the gun down on the bench.

"Come on then boys! Both of you, lets hear it, the world's waiting," Anna pressed.

Ben and I sighed and began to speak at the same time, before she halted us with a raised hand "I don't think so" she unhooked the small pen shaped camera from above her ear and turned it on herself "you all saw it, now watch them humbled before women's natural superiority."

"You said you turned it off," I wailed, appalled that countless thousands had been watching us live, on television. I was still uncomfortable with the newest social fad sweeping the world, and instinctively shied away every time I came across someone wearing one of the small, free cameras that were supplied upon request.

"No need to be shy now, they've been watching the whole time, and now it's time for the money shot, bring it."

I picked up Anna's targets and held them alongside Bens and mine. "As you can all clearly see, Anna beat us in all three rounds, and having never shot a gun before, has proved that men have no natural superiority over women when it comes to shooting."

Thousands, probably tens of thousands of women around the country would be celebrating the world-shaking news.

"Jesus Ben, come on."

The gun was heavy in my pocket, my jacket hanging skewed — Anna's scarf opposite did little to offset the weight of the weapon. I reached in and gripped the gun, taking some of the weight, while my other hand lay amongst the folds of soft material.

I stood, a statue, watching the street, jacket pulled tight, waiting for Ben. Now and then I pulled Anna's scarf out and pressed it to my face. Passers by gave me a wide berth and avoided my eyes — another wasted human, ruined by the world and now invisible to the multitude.

I soon heard the rumble of Ben's old petrol powered Ford. The engine stood out amongst the hum of the many electric cars quietly whirring passed. He pulled up across the street and jumped out of the beaten up blue sedan, searching for me amongst the pedestrians streaming past.

I finally got his attention and he crossed the road at run, narrowly avoiding being hit by a small truck in his haste to reach me. He stood out, even now after being in the city for eight years, his earnest demeanor and lack of guile shone like a beacon in the dark. He was the only human in a city of phantoms, as he had been the day Anna invited him to join us at our table a lifetime ago, all others ignoring him as he searched the packed café for a table.

He enveloped me in a crushing hug and babbled on about the warehouse, of all he had done and all that still remained to do before we left.

We made way for two police officers dragging a sobbing man between them; he begged to all those around him for help. One of the officers flashed a steadfast enforcement badge and the crowd parted.

All eyes turned from the sorry spectacle.

"Did you get one?" Ben asked, in a hushed conspiratorial tone as we walked.

I nodded, leading him into a busy diner and to a table in a dark corner, away from windows and the bustle of families shoveling in a late dinner. I ordered two of the steaks, the flustered waitress took our order and left without once looking up.

I hunched forward and began laying out my plans for the next two days. Ben sat and listened carefully, nodding occasionally and sipping at his mug of black coffee, though never looking me in the eye; I soon tired of it.

"Ben, what is it, what?"

The color drained from his face, his eyes remained glued to the table "Riley, I ... I don't want to ask, but ... What are you going to do when you get her back?"

I leaned away and looked at him as if he were simple "I just told you! I'm taking her away, we're going to disappear for awhile, probably forever."

He shook his head "I know, I remember what you said. That's not what I mean. What about", he paused to clear his throat, "I don't want to say it, I don't believe it either, but what if she *has* taken it?"

The cup I was holding cracked in my hand, spilling hot black coffee across the table. I dropped the shattered porcelain with a hiss and glared across at him, a murderous rage welling inside me. Ben hung his head and cringed, neither daring to meet my gaze or brooch the subject again. I looked away in disgust and locked eyes with an elderly man at the next table, who quickly went back to poking at his half eaten pie.

We sat in a tense silence broken only when the waitress brought our meals; the aroma emanating from the thick steaks sent my stomach growling, but still my anger was all consuming. The waitress noted the tense atmosphere and quickly scraped the shards of porcelain off the table and mopped up the pool of coffee, neither chatting or looking at either of us as she worked. She poured me another cup and left.

A few moments of silence passed before I picked up my fork and began eating methodically. Ben joined me, and soon all tension faded as we gorged ourselves. We soon licked our plates and emptied our coffee. Both of us sat back with eyes half closed, the heavy meal sending us off to a contented torpor.

The waitress ushered us out onto the cold streets long after the other patrons had gone. I waited while Ben fetched his car, absentmindedly running my fingers over the surface of the gun in my coat pocket.

I took another mouthful of stimulants as we pulled into the car park of Ben's small, three-room flat. I waved away his look of concern and followed him up the narrow stairwell. Muffled arguments and blaring television echoed down the hallway until we were inside his small apartment, though the thin walls did little to dampen the dreary cacophony.

The walls, as always, were lined with shelves cluttered with small models of motorbikes and cars from various decades, all painstakingly collected over a lifetime and kept gleaming by incessant polishing. What little wall space left was covered by banners and posters of his favorite makes and models, some even signed by various drivers or other people of note. Why he hadn't restored his old Ford to the same showroom standard as his models was a mystery, though Anna speculated that its current state held some nostalgic significance to him.

He went to bed shortly after, exhausted from twenty hours at the warehouse. Sleep was out of the question for me, my need for it gone now that stimulants coursed though my veins. I spent the night sitting in the small lounge room, holding Anna's scarf to my face, breathing deep of her scent and praying she knew I was coming, that I would never abandon her, even if the world had.

Late in the night a message came through to my cell. I read it a thousand times as I paced the apartment with my fists clenched, waiting for the sun to rise.

"Mateo's out at 9:30 am tomorrow."

9.

I dialed Andrews number before the sun came up.

When his face finally filled the small screen on my cell his eyes were barely open, hair disheveled.

"Riley, it's 5:00" he mumbled, stretching his face and putting his glasses on.

"I need to get moving Andrew. I sent extra, just in case there were other fees or something."

I put the phone down on the kitchen bench, my hands were trembling as I tipped some more stimulants into my mouth and swallowed.

"The money was fine, I'm transferring the remainder back to you this morning. Where are you? You were supposed to drive out to your mothers last night, switch your phone on so she can at least call you Riley."

I shook my head "I'm at a friends. I pick Mateo up when he gets out right? So that's it, he's free?"

Andrew yawned and busied himself with rubbing sleep from the corner of an eye "Not exactly. All I did was get his case transferred to a civil authority, as I did with you. Most of the prisoners in that place shouldn't be there, they're shoving them in there because it's so easy — exactly what I knew would happen under Steadfast. He'll need an attorney to represent him after he's out. He has three weeks until he needs to appear, I'm sure he'll find someone."

I nodded manically as he spoke, not listening to most of it "What about the business?"

"Riley cant we talk about this a little later? "

"No. Just tell me where you're up to and I'll let you go."

He relented with as disdainful scowl "Well, they want the business, but it's as I told you before, desperation is not a good thing when you're selling something. From the information your man Ben sent me yesterday their offer only covers the stock and equipment in the warehouse, let alone the goodwill and standing orders."

"Just get as close to four hundred thousand as you can. I need it done and the money in the bank within three days. Take less if you have to."

He scowled and swore under his breath, unhappy with having his wings clipped.

"Alright, but I'm getting more than that for it Riley. It's not like they don't have money to burn. You know who owns this A Jain Imports? The Peoples Liberation Army. Did you know they're the biggest company in the world now? They own a piece of everything now, we even sold them…"

I held a hand up to silence his raving; none of it mattered to me, not the economic crash, nor the massive financial assistance China had provided to pull us out of it. The Chinese could take over the world for all I cared, or what was left of it now that we'd sucked it dry.

I found some pizza in Ben's fridge and wolfed it down with a few more stimulants, then left a note for him on the kitchen bench. Thirty minutes later I was driving Bens old Ford along the highway out of the city.

. . .

The sun rose in a clear sky, burning away the chill morning air and baking the parched earth. The land was desolate, farmlands abandoned and in ruin. The only rain that had fallen in the last year had burned what remained of the tortured crops, and ended the hope of countless families across much of the country. The radio warned of high UV and I took care to cover what skin was exposed to sunlight.

I passed without issue through the numerous automated toll booths spaced every twenty miles along the freeway. Gaining approval for my trip had been a simple matter once Mateo's bail had been met, and my reason for leaving the city cleared by the relevant authorities. Rarely had Anna or I been denied permission to use the freeways outside the metropolitan area, probably because we were always careful to stick to our approved times and course, and so had never had our travel passes suspended, or our goings-on investigated.

I stopped an hour outside the city at a large service complex and filled the car with six hundred dollars worth of petrol. The prices were absurd, and I wondered, as I often did, why anyone would continue driving petrol powered cars. While the massive increase in registration costs and insurance for the destructive machines had gone some way in reducing their numbers, every second or third car still belched carbon.

A family pulled in beside me while I was topping up the fluids. The wife took two small girls to the restrooms while the husband attached the charger cable. The back of their car was filled with luggage; likely more refugees drawn to the false promise of the city.

The woman soon returned with the children, the girls giggling over their melting ice creams. She hugged her husband and they whispered quietly to each other as the girls finished their treat; they were high on sugar, all life and laughter. The woman cleaned their faces and ushered them into the back seat, bliss as she fussed over her brood.

"Is there a problem?" The man stepped between me and his young family, waving a hand to get my attention, a slightly hostile scowl furrowing his brow.

I mumbled an apology and looked away.

• • •

I turned the radio on as I left the service station, then off, being unwilling to listen to the grizzly details of the latest hurricane in the Gulf, nor the plight of millions left homeless in its wake. It was getting hot and my back was soon wet with sweat, my shirt sticking to the cracked leather seat. The open driver's-side window simply flooded the car with hot, dry wind, though it cooled sweat-covered skin. The air conditioning I saved for later, the old car would only produce an hour of cold at most. I was careful to keep hydrated as I drove.

An hour later I called Andrew and followed his directions through a small town near its end. Most businesses were boarded up, weatherboard houses sat decaying and abandoned. A few withered old women shuffled down the empty main street, all turning to stare as I passed.

Soon the ruined settlement was lost in the shimmering heat haze, a well-maintained road taking me north through a boulder strewn wasteland of cracked earth and skeletal trees. In time even their bleached bones became scarce, an endless expanse of tortured red earth stretching to the horizon.

A figure emerged from the dust and haze ahead, stumbling with eyes covered and head hung, tattooed skin glistening with sweat. He flinched when he heard the car approaching and stepped off the searing bitumen.

I got out and quickly led him to the passenger seat, giving him a pair of dark sunglasses. Even then he winced when opening his eyes; the light of day too harsh, his underground imprisonment too long.

He gulped the water I handed him, spilling much of it down his front and coughing more onto the dash. His hands were shaking, skin blistered by the sun. The remainder of the bottle he tipped over his head, shaking like a dog and gasping.

"Jesus I didn't know you were coming, no one told me shit" Mateo mumbled, his throat raw "I waited in the bus shelter for hours, thought I'd fucking die out there!"

I turned the car around, away from the small shelter far in the distance, and the prison beyond; hidden deep under the barren moonscape, its location unknown and unseen by few but its builders.

Mateo leaned back, eyes closed, sighing as the air-conditioning blasted ice over burning skin.

"Got a smoke?"

I handed him a pack and lighter. He smoked the entire cigarette in rapture. It was soon gone, and he drained a second bottle of water before lighting another. The blighted landscape blurred past as he looked out the window. He muttered in Spanish for a few moments and crossed his chest, before turning to me with a puff of smoke, a grin lighting his scarred face.

"Time to get your lady, eh."

10.

We stopped at the same service station I had used earlier that morning. The small diner was empty, save for a young couple eating and chatting quietly in a corner. Dishes clanked and music blared from the kitchen.

A girl, no more than sixteen, came laughing from the kitchen; her smile vanished as she laid eyes on Mateo. She retreated behind the counter, her frantic sorting of napkins betraying her fear. We took a seat and I waved her over, as if coaxing a frightened animal. She took our order with shaking hands and head hung; Mateo's dark eyes never left her.

Sickly sweet strawberry lingered in the air when she left.

"Thought I'd never see one of those again," he mumbled around a fresh cigarette.

I glanced at the retreating waitress, all sounds of mirth from the kitchen faded as she disappeared within. The couple in the corner of the diner had stopped eating and spoke in whispers. Both kept their eyes on the table in front of them.

Mateo lent back in his chair; a tattooed demon billowing smoke from his nose "I have to see my family today. You need to drop me off there, I can talk to my uncle tonight."

"You're sure he can do this? What if he's not ready?"

"You saved a draft message in the email I gave you right?"

"Yes"

"Has it been deleted?"

I nodded.

"That means he's ready. He's in the zone all the time, makes some good cash from it. Have you checked the email again for any others drafts?"

"There haven't been any."

"Don't worry, if it's deleted it means he's ready, just waiting for you to give him details. I'll sort it with him"

I nodded again, letting out a lungful of air; the past few days of stress, of not knowing, had taken their toll.

"Have you been in there?" I asked quietly.

He shook his head and flicked his cigarette butt to the floor "No, but don't worry — Cesar owns it."

The girl came back with our meals, pale and demure, her eyes never left the floor. We ate in silence, Mateo devoured his meal and half of mine in minutes.

She never returned with our check, nor would I, had I been her. I left more than enough on the table and we left. The young couple in the corner were silent, heads hung as we passed.

. . .

The neighborhood Mateo directed me through was everything I expected it to be; destitute and doomed.

We drove past burnt-out buildings and a school in ruins. Children played amongst the wreckage of destroyed cars, while old men and women shuffled like ghosts along the sidewalk. The sky was darkening as we turned into a side street and pulled over. I ducked as an army helicopter roared overhead, cutting a straight line across the slums. Mateo didn't seem to notice as he flung the car door open and tore up the front steps of a squat cement house. He yelled in Spanish and disappeared inside. I thought better of following and stood by the car, waiting for him to return for me.

News of Mateo's arrival spread like wildfire through the slums, the small cement porch of his mother's house filling with well-wishers. Carloads of tattooed men in gang colors roared into the street, many of them with military issue rifles slung over their shoulders or pistols stuffed into jeans. I was careful to keep my eyes to the ground, and ignored their hostile stares as they passed. Young mothers came with giggling children, their broods hooting and running through the legs of adults. The elderly were treated with great respect by all, and they, in turn, doted on babies and children, or shared drinks with armed gang members.

Every one seemed to know one another, or if they didn't it seemed not to matter, and I soon realized that for all its poverty and violence, the neighborhood in which I stood had something mine did not. For where I had returned to a silent apartment surrounded by suspicious neighbors; Mateo came back to a community, he came back to a home.

It was dark when he finally emerged from his mothers house, followed by a horde of chattering family and friends. Mateo was swaying drunkenly as he threw an arm over my shoulders and introduced me to the crowd; the horde enveloped me and swept me into the house. I was hugged by an endless procession of teary-eyed old ladies, and thumped on the back by jubilant gang members and excited, grubby-faced children.

I refused their offers of drinks at first, until the pressure became so much that I relented, gulping down a fiery shot of tequila in the packed living room. The crowd cheered its approval. A group of squealing children tore through the room, one of them tripped over in front of me. A young women pulled the squirming boy to his feet and laughed as she led him outside by the hand. Three other young mothers followed, all of them giggling and chatting amongst themselves.

I broke, turning my head in shame as I wept. I don't know why the sight of the mother and child affected me so, and I waved the crowd to leave me — but they would not. It felt as if a hundred hands patted me on the back and another shot of Tequila was put in my hand.

Mateo's small, but ferocious mother, became my guardian through the night, bringing an endless stream of grateful friends and family to share a shot of tequila with her sons savior. The night blurred, I raved of Anna to any who would listen, shared drink with Mateo and his circle, many of them brandishing guns and roaring as he boasted of our plan. They took their shirts off and explained some of their greater achievements, their lives forever gouged into skin by blade and needle. Mateo cut a small crescent into his forearm; blood his oath, ink upon the scar would reward success.

Mateo soon left with a carload of his peers, promising to see his uncle and to call me in the morning. I stumbled across the yard and collapsed on the back seat of Bens car, Anna's scarf my pillow.

. . .

I awoke in the sweltering mid-morning sun, my throat parched and head splitting. The street resembled a war zone after the night's festivities. Cans and broken bottles littered the road and sidewalk. Here and there lay those who had still not woken, the sight akin to the images of the disaster I had seen five years ago; bodies lying abandoned in the glaring sunshine.

I took a swig of the water bottle Ben carried in the car in case of radiator problems, gagging as I swallowed the hot, tangy liquid. I stumbled to the house, shielding my eyes from the glare.

My head pounded as I knocked on the front door, setting a dog barking inside. Mateo's mother ushered me in and sat me at the kitchen table, babbling away in heavily accented English while she tried to find something to feed me.

"You brought me my boy. You know it's the second time they take him from me. I knew he'd come back, just like the first time. They try to make him white. Did you know? Government took him from me when he was a baby like all the others, but he always comes back. No government can break family, family is always stronger, family will win"

I poked at the eggs and toast she cooked while she called one person after another in an effort to locate Mateo.

When she finally found him her tone had darkened. They began to argue immediately; she handed me the phone with murder in her eyes.

Mateo sounded tired and hung over, though relaxed "Good party eh. Mum says she fed you, that's good. She'll draw you a map to my uncles place. Don't worry if she gives you shit. I'll see you here."

He hung up and I handed the phone back to his scowling mother. She moved around the table and sat opposite me. Her voice was quiet, though she trembled slightly "What are you doing with my boy?"

I was unsure of what I should tell her and answered quietly, my eyes avoiding hers "He's helping me with something, that's all."

She stood from the table, anger contorting her face.

"And what does Cesar have to do with it? I told my boy I don't want him seeing my brother. It's Cesar's fault he tattooed his face like all the others" she yelled,"It's because of his uncle he gets into trouble, he's a good boy!"

She was a tiny woman, but her eyes hinted at a vast capacity for fighting, beyond anything I could muster in my state. I held both palms towards her and stood from the table.

"Please, Mateo's the only one I know who can help. I don't know what else to do. Please, just give me the directions to Cesar and I'll leave."

She stuck a finger in my face, "I smell death on you, nothing good ever comes from you people. What do you need from him that you can't get somewhere else? You get out, get out of my house!" she screamed.

I rushed through the house, followed by a tirade of abuse that set the dog barking again. She followed and stood on the porch, yelling and cursing as I fumbled to open the car door. The old Ford took a long time to start, and her tirade echoed down the street until the engine roared to life.

The tires screeched and I pulled away. Panic took hold almost immediately as I realized I had no way of contacting Mateo. I pulled over down the street along side two young men sitting with their heads hung, vomit marring the sidewalk by their feet. I recognized them from the party, neither had gang tattoos, but I had seen them drinking with those who did.

"Eh its Mateo's pet white boy" they mumbled, pushing themselves to their feet and staggering towards the car "you given us a ride or what?"

They hopped in, one on the back seat and the other up front beside me — I nearly retched from the stench of sweat and vomit that wafted into the car with them.

"Sweet ride bro, full petrol and all eh," the alpha next to me remarked. He ran his hands over the dash and opened the glove box, pulling out a crumpled pack of cigarettes Mateo had stashed away. He lit one and passed another to his companion in the back. I declined the same offer with a raised hand and he put the pack in his top pocket

"Where're you going?" I asked.

"Three blocks, easy. Give this beast some blast! Come on, hit it bro," he said with a puff, resting a foot on the dash.

"You know the way to Cesar's?" I asked, putting the car back in gear.

All color drained from the boys face, he glanced back to his deathly silent friend, then to me. He no longer looked at me as if I were simple.

"What you want Cesar for?" He asked quietly.

"I have some business with him, I'm meeting Mateo there."

"I didn't know you were with Cesar." He took his foot down and put the pack of cigarettes back in the glove box, then drew a map on Ben's registration papers. He explained it in great detail, while his friend lent over and corrected him now and then on the most efficient way to navigate through the slums.

After confirming I would find my way they both got out and closed the doors respectfully behind them.

"Don't worry, our place isn't on the way" he said, waving me on.

I left them stumbling down the road, their reaction to my mention of Mateo's uncle knotting my stomach. The map they had given me took me into the heart of the slums, deeper than any who wished to return would willingly go.

11.

Cesar sat opposite me in a small tin shack, a half-empty bottle of thirty year old Glenfiddich between us on the rusted metal table, alongside two disassembled handguns and a pile of oily rags. Behind him sat two shirtless gang members playing cards on a oil drum turned coffee table — one had a compact machine gun strapped tight across his back.

Others toiled in the warehouse proper behind me, assembling weapons and packing them into crates. None of the tattooed gang members seemed to care that I saw; they feared no government reprisals, such was their power in the slums.

I was afraid, anyone would be, but I tried not to show it. I reminded myself that life had already taken from me the only thing that mattered; that there was nothing these men could do that I feared.

My best guess was that Cesar had to be nearly fifty; much older than the gang members I had seen so far. He was short and thickset, the same tattoos and scars that Mateo wore so proudly covered his uncle. Little of his skin could be seen under the dark ink, and only then it was largely scar tissue; none of the old wounds crisscrossing his thick torso and arms looked to have been cut in deliberately, as I had seen Mateo do at the party.

"Mateo says your wife took it eh," Cesar said, rubbing his bearded chin and nodding his shaved head to his nephew behind me. Sweat beaded on the dark symbols gouged into his forehead.

"They took her away. They said she took it." I replied, my jaw tight.

"And you don't think she did. And now you want her back."

I nodded.

He took a gulp of whiskey from the bottle, absent mindedly scratching at an old bullet wound on the side of his chest. "I don't do that. I got contacts all around — people want to send something in there it comes through me; letters, medicine. I don't bring people out."

He took another mouthful and hacked phlegm to the side.

"I'm willing to pay well to get her out. I've sold everything to get the money I have. I'm sure Mateo has told you how much I can pay."

He leaned back and stroked his wiry goatee. "He told me, but I don't see the point."

"She's my wife, that's the point." I held his gaze, fist clenched under the table.

Cesar shot a glance to Mateo standing behind me "The point, my friend, is that if she took it, it's a waste of time getting her out. I've seen what that shit does to people.

And what happens when the cops find you walking around with someone they just dumped in the Zone? That'll ruin my business friend. Maybe best if you forget."

I shook my head and took a deep breath to calm myself, "That won't be a problem, I've made arrangements. I'm taking her out of the country. We wont be coming back."

He raised an eyebrow, the movement contorted a sequence of numbers and symbols above his eye "Is that right? You just take her away, huh? Tell me friend — how you going to do that? What, you got friends on the border?"

"That's my business, I've organized all the documents I need. It's taken care of. We won't be found, I promise you that."

He watched me with dark eyes before whispering to the men behind him. They chuckled and glanced over to me, murmuring in Spanish and shaking their heads as they returned to their game. "You know what we do around here if one of our people takes it?" He rested a thick, tattooed arm on the table. A flicker of sadness in his eyes betrayed the overt show of bravado, "We put a bullet in their head. It's better for them, better for everyone."

"Do we have a deal or not, Cesar?"

A smirk crept onto his scarred face, "You are a business man eh! That's good, but you better be tougher than you look if you think you're coming."

"I'm getting her back Cesar, and if you can't or won't help then tell me now and I'll find someone else. I don't have time for this shit."

The smirk left his face. Mateo stepped to the side as Cesar and I locked eyes, neither of us willing to back down. Our standoff lasted long enough for the men behind Cesar to shuffle nervously. One of them rearranged a pistol stuffed in his jeans and glanced from me to his companion.

Cesar nodded and leaned back, arms behind his head as he let out a soft whistle. "Must be some woman, friend. Must be some kind of women for this shit."

"She's everything." I whispered. For a moment I was somewhere else, somewhere beautiful.

We sat for a few more moments, reading what we could from one another until he nodded, taking another drink from the bottle and insisting I do likewise. I gulped a mouthful, the Whiskey molten gold burning through me.

A moment later Cesar stood and offered his hand; I pushed my chair back and did likewise.

· · ·

I made my way out of the slums with great difficulty, the mapping system inset into the dash of the Ford was woefully inadequate and I switched the screen off with a mumbled curse. Many streets ended with abandoned roadblocks, some with destroyed police cars scattered in front of them. I even passed the rusted remains of a downed helicopter, though it had been so thoroughly stripped it was almost unrecognizable.

I was navigating around an upturned bus when Ben called. I pulled over as his flushed face filled the screen on my cell "Riley, where've you been? It's been crazy over here. Your lawyer was here this morning."

He was near breathless by the time I slowed him down with a raised hand "I'm just organizing things. How did it go?"

"Your lawyer, Andrew, he said they're buying the business. He wouldn't tell me how much, but he said you'd be very happy."

"Good, you need to be ready by tomorrow Ben."

He nodded and let out a lungful of air, "I'm ready."

Though his face was small on the screen it was still easy to see the color drain from it.

"I'll see you tonight."

I hung up and started dialing my mothers number.

"Hey, nice car man."

I jumped and turned to see a grinning brown face, topped by a dirty red baseball cap, leaning in through the open window. He was young, barely a man, though obviously the alpha of the two cronies standing behind him. He reached through the open window and snatched the keys from the ignition before I had time to react.

"Hey, settle down, pendejo, we just want to see your car that's all."

I reached for the gun under my jacket on the passenger seat, but they were fast, the three of them pulled me from the car and threw me to the ground with little effort. Alpha laughed and shoved me backwards as I scrambled to my feet, "No one's here to help you white boy. What you going to do now eh?"

I held my palms towards him in a show of submission "I don't want any trouble. Keep the car, I don't give a shit, just let me get some things out."

I barely saw his hands move. The world exploded white, the next moment I was lying on my side in the dirt. My ears roared and blood filled my mouth. I watched from far away as they each light a cigarette and inspected their new car.

The leader threw Anna's scarf around his neck, to the amusement of his friends, who roared with laughter. I growled and pushed myself to my hands and knees. A foot landed in my stomach, driving the wind from me; another and I curled into a ball as blows rained down from all directions.

My head snapped to the side and the world was no more.

"This is my spot, right here."

Anna snuggled her head into my chest, her long black hair cool on sweat-covered skin. Wind and rain lashed the world outside; nothing could touch us.

I stroked her hair as she trailed her fingers across my chest, goose bumps prickling my skin.

"We're going to leave all of this you know. We promised we would" she whispered.

I hugged her closer and kissed the top of her head, both of us slowly drifting to sleep as the storm howled through the city.

"I hope it never stops" she murmured. Her words slurred as sleep took her.

I glanced to the window. The rain was heavy, water was streaming down the glass. Likely the world would be better off without it, my skin was still red where the water had touched me earlier- only the hardiest plants, or those sprayed down in the morning, would survive it.

"Just sleep," I whispered, stroking her hair. My stomach knotted as the storm rattled the windows "don't worry about any of it."

PART II

12.

"You stay close, understand? And keep the torches moving. Their eyes are sensitive to it, it'll keep them back."

I nodded to Cesar's instructions, taking a deep breath to steady myself before I pulled the gas mask over my face and tightened the straps. Mateo and Cesar's cousin, Omar, did the same. I shuddered at the sight of the army issue masks, a nightmare of the future.

My stomach churned, both hands trembling slightly.

The double doors of the convention centre were closed behind Cesar, though still the low drone of thousands could be heard, punctuated now and then by screams. I looked to Mateo standing at my side, his knuckles were white around a loaded gun. He nodded, a jerking, almost spasmodic motion — the boy was terrified, though doing his best to hide it from his uncle.

Around us sat countless empty food crates stretching far out into the car park, and amongst them, laying where they had fallen, were the decaying bodies of men and women.

Cesar spoke again, his voice small and metallic through the earpiece of my mask. "Remember, these people are scared, and desperate — you don't let any of them near you or we could be swamped. Once they get too far gone they're dangerous, understand?"

I nodded again and clutched Anna's scarf in my coat pocket.

If there is a god, bring her back to me, I beg you.

Cesar chambered a round in each of his pistols and put them back in his chest holster, then mumbled a quick prayer in Spanish and crossed his chest. Mateo and Omar did likewise.

He nodded to each of us one last time, then pulled the doors open and disappeared within.

. . .

It was pitch black inside, our torches solid beams in the void. The voices of thousands echoed around us — screams, shouting, weeping — the sound of hell. The domed ceiling of the convention centre was lost in the inky blackness far above, the stench of death and decay powerful, despite the heavy filters in the mask.

We were barely five metres in and already I was struggling to control my breathing. Panic threatened to take hold, and had I not had Anna's scarf gripped tight in my left hand it might have. I blinded myself to all but finding her, every time fear clutched at my stomach I imagined her scared and alone, somewhere within the vast domed building.

Cesar and his cousin Omar moved ahead, with Mateo and I keeping as close as possible. I saw nothing for a few moments, then, ghosts in the dark. They were few at first, grey shapes flittering on the edge of our torchlight.

Soon we were surrounded.

Hundreds of people emerged from the dark as we moved deeper inside. Many wept with their hands outstretched and begged for our help.

Omar and Cesar roared and waved their torches across the faces of the encroaching crowd. People retreated into the darkness, shielding their eyes and cringing, though many tried to come towards us regardless. Some of the men and women looked normal, though their clothes were filthy. Others were thin and scab covered, little left of their hair.

A thick set man wearing a stained shirt and tie emerged from the dark at Cesar's side. He begged for help before Cesar pushed him violently away, a gun stuffed in his face. Mateo and I stepped around the large man as he sank to his knees and wept.

Many of those who pleaded for our help were women, some of them so weak they were held up by others, or crawled on the urine covered floor — the sight nearly broke me. Had Mateo not pressed his back to mine and urged me to move faster it might have. I looked to his uncle ahead and moved closer. Mateo, my appointed protector, grasped at my jacket as if he feared I would leave him behind.

We soon began stepping over bodies. Emaciated corpses of men and women lay strewn about, laying where they had fallen, to decay amongst the living. Omar lead us deeper into the nightmare, and to my horror I realised that many of the bodies on the floor were not corpses. Those that still lived lay with eyes glazed, their last breaths soon to come, and to my shame I stepped over them as if they were dead already.

Everywhere I turned I saw either the dead and dying, or those still strong enough to plead for help. All of them we left to be taken by the dark, their voices drowned out by the multitude. I avoided looking into the eyes of those we passed and picked up my pace, coming close to running into Cesar as panic nearly took me.

The tiered seating above us rumbled as more people moved down onto the floor of the convention centre, our arrival drawing the poor people like moths to a flame.

Omar lead us deeper into the packed building, stepping around a group of men and women huddled together on the floor; some prayed, while others simply sat with heads hung, crying softly in the dark. Mateo crossed his chest and began to pray as well, his mantra wavered whenever torchlight illuminated some new horror.

My eyes went from one face to another until my heart jumped at the sight of long dark hair — the women was a stranger, her skin scab covered. She fell to her knees and stretched her hands out to me, "Help us, please god help us. I have children outside, help me."

I moved my torch on and the void swallowed her as if she never was — a moment later I pulled my mask off and vomited to the side, as if retching my very soul out.

"Keep moving and stay close" Cesar ordered in a calm voice.

He signalled Mateo to move closer to me, "I told you to watch him boy."

I wiped my mouth with the back of my hand and pulled my mask back down. Anna's scarf in my coat pocket was wet with sweat, though still I gripped it in my fist. I whispered a quick prayer to the universe for strength and let out a long breath.

Omar stepped around a pile of empty crates, the food they held long since devoured. He glanced at a photo of Anna stuck to his rifle then back to the crowd before him.

He shook his head and moved on.

Deeper and deeper we went; the bright morning outside and the teeming city beyond the wall an impossible reality. I spat a curse to the millions and their apathy, to the malls and the music, to the greed and vanity.

We soon began moving up through the tiered seating, followed by more people pleading for help. Mateo drove them back whenever they came too close, roaring and waving his torch from face to face, and when necessary, lashing out with his feet and fists to drive them off. The poor people screamed and tumbled away into the dark. Everyone of them was someone's father or mother, son or daughter — I doubted the god Mateo continually called to would ever forgive us.

Countless bodies were strewn about the rows of tiered seating, some in advance stages of decay. Many sat upright in seats, bloated and staring into the void before them.

Others lay on the stairs, curled as if in the womb. We soon reached the top of the seating, the sound from below like some great hive of misery.

At a signal from Cesar we turned our torches off and flicked a switch on the side of the masks — Mateo and I gasped as the night vision equipment flared to life. Thousands languished below — though still the dead in the seating outnumbered the living they held vigil over.

The world flashed white as Omar fired into the air, driving back the crowd that had followed us up and was now converging on us. The burst of automatic gunfire was deafening; many of the poor people tripped and tumbled down the stairs as they scrambled to get away.

Cesar's cousin kept the multitude at bay as we scanned for any sign of my Anna.

"This Cesar, he's done it before right? He's got someone out of the Zone?" Ben asked. The city at night was a blur of lights as millions bustled about their futile concerns. He brought the old Ford to a squeaking stop at a set of lights. A convoy of police vehicles and personnel carriers raced by, lights flashing.

"No, he's never brought anyone out" I said, my voice distant.

The lights changed and we pulled away, a chopper roaring overhead.

"I don't like it Riley. The slums are dangerous. The cops don't even go in there anymore, only the army. You should have taken me when you met him, you could have been killed."

I shrugged, "Well I wasn't, they had their fun and left, I'll be fine."

He glanced to my battered face *"Left without taking the car? Riley tell me what happened. Was it this Cesar that did that to you?"*

I exploded, my rage genuine, my words lies *"Jesus Ben I told you! They dragged me from the car and beat the shit out of me and left, it's not important anymore."*

"Alright, I believe you. Just calm down. But from now on I don't leave your side, not until she's back ok? ... Riley!"

I nodded.

We drove through the night in silence for a time, the weight of the coming day heavy. Ben cleared his throat as we crossed the river, the exclusion zone black in a sea of light, *"So his cousin comes in with us, the one in the army?"*

"He's stationed on the wall, he'll meet us in the sewers. Mateo's coming as well. Once we're in we go to Cesar's safe house to drop supplies, then to the convention centre."

"And if Anna's not in there?"

"Then we search the streets, building by building if we have to. We don't leave until we find her."

Two helicopters flew along the river in the distance, search lights tracking the riverbank. The thump of rotors was heavy in my stomach.

"Did he say how many?" Ben asked, his voice quiet.

I shook my head, my eyes glued to the window and the dark area along the river. We passed a woman walking with two children, the night was still young, her brood hooting as they tore along the footpath.

"Too many" I said, looking away from the happy scene and back to the choppers speeding along the river bank, *"too many."*

Mateo was the last to crawl through the hole in the wall, bolting the metal plate into place and throwing his pack across the room. Rubbish piled against the walls and around the makeshift kitchen, the furniture decaying and scant. I staggered to a rat-eaten couch and sat heavily, my head hung, eyes distant.

"Boy, make some food," Cesar grumbled, taking his shirt off and gulping from a bottle of whiskey. He sat at the small table and placed his two pistols in front of him along with a deck of cards, which he began shuffling. A scowl contorted his face, his manner that of a man with little experience in failure.

Omar had seen us to the safe house then returned to his unit on the wall.

"Don't worry friend, we find her tomorrow. Come have a drink" Cesar pushed the bottle across the table and kicked a chair out, the cards in his hand forgotten.

"I didn't know there'd be so many" I whispered, looking back to the floor at my feet.

He shook his head and took another drink from the bottle "it's getting worse. I've never seen it like that."

"We cant go back out tonight?" I asked, looking the bolted steel plate, sealing us in the small, two-room apartment.

"No. They stay indoors because the suns too bright, you saw their eyes right? Poor bastards cant handle it once they're too far gone."

I nodded, seeing again the pleading, swollen red eyes and scab covered skin of those sheltering in the convention centre. Every one of them would be dead within a month or so, forgotten and left to rot in the dark.

"The streets are easy in the day, but night's different. A lot of people come out, wandering round and trying for a way out or looking for food. We'd be swamped if they saw us, maybe we'd have to shoot people."

His two pistols sat next to the bottle, the light of electric lanterns glinted off cold steel. My throat tightened and I shook my head, looking away. "No, we're not killing anyone."

He shrugged and offered the bottle of whiskey to me again "Sure you don't want a drink?"

I ignored him, running my fingers over the photo of Anna. Whatever he mumbled under his breath was in Spanish, his attention soon turning to Mateo, who was serving stew into three bowls. The bottle of whiskey disappeared quickly, along with his dinner.

Mateo sat beside me on the couch, both of us poking at the stew, haunted by the days search.

"How could there be so many?" he whispered "I thought it was getting better."

No one answered him, the only sound was Cesar slurping the last from his bowl then scraping the leftovers from the pot. Soon after he stumbled past and collapsed on a ragged mattress opposite. He looked at me through narrow eyes and spoke with a heavy tongue, "Would have been better if your friend came. Better with more people that know her" he said, his dark eyes bored into me.

"Yes", I looked away, my voice near breaking "It would have been better."

13.

I left Ben sitting in the living room organizing our supplies, closing the door to his small bedroom and sitting on the edge of the bed. The bag I had packed for Anna was small: a few items of clothing, vitamins, her favorite perfume, a ring given to her by her grandmother and other such items too dear to part with.

Once packed there was little else to do but wait for the morning- everything else was done. The money from the business had been cleared and dealt with, a deposit had been paid to Cesar, supplies had been bought.

Her scarf was the only item I left unpacked. I sat with the long length of blue material across my lap, running my fingers over the soft wool. There were small imperfections here and there, knots and breaks in the weave; each one a little of Anna forever entwined in thread. I smiled when I came across these, remembering the mumbled profanities such mistakes would often bring; the scarf might be put aside for days, sometimes *weeks until she'd forgiven herself enough to continue with her project.*

Ben knocked softly on the door and entered, sitting beside me on the edge of the bed. He looked tired, dark rings encircled his eyes. Neither of us spoke, the magnitude of the coming day weighed heavy upon both of us. Twice he looked about to speak, only to shake his head and look back to the floor between his feet.

I was about to suggest he go and get some sleep when he began chuckling quietly to himself. "Sorry ... I was just thinking about that dog," he shook his head, "you think it's still alive?"

"We owe her for that, huh?" I whispered.

"Last time I go skinny dipping and leave my clothes with someone like Anna," he was laughing now.

A smile touched my face, "We kind of asked for it though- we shouldn't have pushed her. I cant believe we waited so long, I knew she wouldn't come back. I should have known when I saw that look in her eye. I swear to god that dog was the oldest thing I've ever seen- barked like an old man coughing," I laughed.

Ben was in hysterics

"Can you imagine if someone saw us, two naked guys carrying a fat, half-dead Labrador across a field?" he said, wiping his eyes as he struggled to regain his breath.

"We couldn't leave him laying there! Poor old guy didn't have an ounce of quit in him. He must have chased us for over a mile before he hit the dirt."

Ben bent over, laughter flushing his face, "Remember when we finally got to your mum's? Anna and your brothers waiting for us with the camera. We still have to get her back for that!"

Our laughter left as quickly as it had come, an awkward silence filled the small room. Ben nodded to himself and rested a hand on my shoulder as he stood.

"We'll get her back Riley."

I nodded and looked back to the scarf, kneading the thick blue wool.

"Try to get some rest ok."

I nodded again.

He paused at the door for a moment, then closed it behind him. A moment later the tap began running in the kitchen and dishes clanked- Ben would not leave an untidy house behind should we not return. I locked the bedroom door and sat back on the bed. I wanted a few hours privacy before we left in the morning, and knew Ben would find an excuse to come and talk again.

The front door burst open seconds later and heavy footsteps thumped into the living room. I leapt from the bed and froze as a sickeningly familiar voice filled the apartment outside. "Going on a trip are we?"

"Who are you? Get the hell out of my house!" Ben roared, I heard him stomping from the kitchen towards the front door.

"Stay right there Ben, take another step and you're done. You see the badge? It means you do as you're told. We're looking for your friend Riley. He's been doing the strangest things lately, moving money around, going in and out of the slums, spending time with terrible people Ben."

I backed away from the door, eyeing my jacket at the end of the bed. Adrenalin was coursing through me, my muscles began to shake from the rapid buildup of energy.

"I don't know anything about what he's been doing, I haven't seen him" Ben answered, even thick with anger his voice betrayed him.

"Really, so he hasn't been driving around in your car huh? You didn't meet him outside a shooting gallery a few nights ago? Well done Ben, you just lied yourself into three months for interfering with a Steadfast Enforcement. Give me a few more, lets go for six shall we?"

Heavy footsteps thumped across the living room and stopped outside the bedroom door, the handle turned.

"Locked" another voice yelled.

I backed away, futilely looking around for an escape- four solid walls with no window and only one door offered none. Desperation decided my next course of action; one I would regret for the rest of my life.

I pulled the Berretta from my coat pocket and whispered a prayer to the universe as the door burst open.

We slunk along the sidewalk, keeping to the shade when we could. Even at such an early hour a heat haze hung over the abandoned streets. Bodies, freshly dead, lay bloated in the sun. Others were nothing but rags on dried bones and leathery skin, scattered across the street by scavengers and time.

I walked with Anna's scarf gripped in my pocket, a talisman against the horrors of the zone.

I'm coming babe, you have to know I'm coming.

We moved in silence, every slide of debris or scuttle of rat had Mateo and I jumping; Cesar walked as if he were strolling through a park. Both of his guns were holstered, the dirty white singlet he wore was wet with sweat, though he seemed otherwise oblivious to the heat.

His cousin Omar walked slightly ahead of us, his assault rifle slung over his shoulder, sweat darkening the back and armpits of his army camouflage. He constantly held a hand to his earpiece so as to monitor the activities of his peers on the wall and beyond, while he scanned the surrounding buildings with an infra-red eyepiece. Now and then he would usher us under cover where we would wait until helicopters roared overhead, low and fast, their shadows blinking in the glaring sunlight.

"Do they land in here?" I whispered to Cesar as we hunkered in the dark of a small convenience store. Omar moved further into the shadows and listened to the chatter of the pilots.

"No, just drop food and go." Cesar said. He waited for a nod from Omar before waving for us to leave the shadows. We crept out onto the sidewalk, shielding our eyes until they adjusted to the glare.

Omar led us past a small café and continued scanning the surrounding buildings, occasionally adjusting his eyepiece as he sought signs of life. The silence sat heavy, broken only by the occasional squawk of a distant crow or scuttling rats.

I moved closer to Cesar, Mateo as always my shadow.

"So the army never comes in here?" I asked in a low voice.

Cesar answered without turning, his eyes scanning the streets and buildings around us as we walked. "Sometimes. Omar keeps an ear out, no one in here today."

We walked in silence for a time, following Omar as he continued scanning. Soon he raised a hand, calling us to a stop as he adjusted focus, the scanner he wore hummed as he turned up the power. The building he had in his sights was a dilapidated four story apartment at the end of the block. Rags and upturned tables blocked the windows, weeds were taking hold in cracked mortar. He waved us forward, pointing to the structure and speaking in Spanish to Cesar, who quickly translated.

"Maybe twenty up there, top floors. Some nearly dead, not much heat left in them."

We crossed the street and kept to the shadows as we moved towards the apartment building, my heart near ripping from my chest. I stumbled many times, my eyes were glued to the looming structure and not my footing.

We were half way there when Mateo stopped, shielding his eyes and peering down the street, "What's that?"

I saw nothing, the glare was too strong; the shimmering air blurring the distance.

Omar and Cesar joined us, both peering down the street and whispering to one another. Omar hissed for silence and adjusted his eyepiece. A moment later he swore under his breath and barked a command in Spanish.

"Inside, now!" Cesar ordered, waving us after him.

We ducked into a burned out pharmacy. Cesar quickly checked the rear for danger as we squatted behind a pile of upturned shelving and waited for the roar of a chopper that never came.

Cesar began whispering to his cousin, only to be silenced by a another hiss and raised hand from a scowling Omar.

"What is it?" I whispered to Mateo. He was barely visible in the gloom beside me, only the occasional patch of tattooed skin and white of eye flashed in the dark.

"Just listen man, you hear that?" he whispered, holding a finger to his mouth to silence me.

A moment later I too heard it - the sound of a women crying, small and distant, drifted in from the street; I would have leapt to my feet had Cesar not been there to restrain me.

"Wait friend, we wait and see."

Soon voices could be heard, along with the scuff of shoes on cement. I peered through a football sized hole in the crumbling plaster to the sidewalk beyond, my heart near breaking as the weeping grew nearer.

A women, perhaps in her fifties, walked by, hugging herself as she sobbed, her eyes squinting against the glare of the sun. Others followed, men and women of all ages and races, their clothes clean, skin clear. Some held onto each other as they walked, others stumbled alone, staring about in shock as they trailed after the main group.

"Just dumped in here," Cesar whispered "we're close to a gate. They go to the convention center first, some stay there, others try the buildings. If they see us they'll want help. Stay quiet friend, there's nothing we can do."

The ragged group soon passed, the last, an old women who struggled to keep up. Her white hair was tightly curled into a perm, the clothes she wore looked suited to sleeping or shuffling around a retirement home — she looked anything other than a drug addict. She stopped and rested a moment, her trembling hands shielding her eyes from the glare before she moved on after the others.

"Old ones don't last long," Cesar said softly, shaking his head and mumbling a curse to those who would do such a thing. The compassion in his voice surprised me.

Omar waited a few minutes before he crept outside and checked the streets for stragglers, then called us out after him. The old woman was far in the distance. By the time my eyes had adjusted to the glare she was little but a ghost in the shimmering haze.

Mateo rested a hand on my shoulder, "Leave them man, they're already dead."

A moment later the Zone swallowed her and I turned away, as had the world.

• • •

The Berretta dropped to the floor, my hand, my entire being, numb. My ears rang from the roar of the weapon, my wrists still vibrated from the kick of the ten rounds I had fired out the bedroom door. Orange-hair lay gurgling on the floor, both hands grasping his torn throat. His foot jerked back and forth, smearing his blood, and that of his two dead peers, across the polished cement floor.

Soon his gurgling ceased and his leg stiffened, and still I stood, a trembling hand covering my mouth. I don't know how long I remained frozen in place, it might have been minutes only, it might have been an hour. Long enough for the sight of what I had done to forever burn itself into my soul. I would see it every time I closed my eyes for the rest of my life.

A distant siren roused me to action and I backed towards the front door, my eyes locked on Ben lying strewn across the couch. Blood covered his face, running from the single wound in his forehead - none of the three intervention officers lying dead on the floor had had a chance to fire their weapons.

"I'm sorry, Jesus Ben I'm sorry."

The convention center had been chaos, thousands screaming, begging and dying. Here, in the dilapidated building, nothing but whispers in the dark, distant moaning and the scuttle of rats.

Omar and Mateo searched the rooms on one side of the hallway, Cesar and I the other. I followed him through the door and stepped over the bodies of a man and women laying with their arms around each other. Perhaps they had died a few days ago, their bodies were already beginning to bloat. Cesar simply stepped over them without so much as a glace, I tried to do the same and failed. I looked long enough for them to be forever burned into my memory. Whoever they had been, they had at least found some comfort in each other before they died.

There were others in the living room, two men and a women sitting huddled together, mumbling quietly in the dark. None of them looked up when we entered, whether they were ignoring us, or their minds were so far gone they didn't know we were there, was impossible to tell.

"Careful," Cesar warned, his pistol trained upon the trembling group, "their minds are gone."

We moved past them, deeper into the apartment. Cesar moved with caution, gun held before him, his finger squeezed the trigger so tightly it must have been atoms from firing. The doors to the two bedrooms stood open, and I followed him into the first. The mattress had been upturned against the window, blocking most sunlight, the cupboards tipped on the floor and smashed. The second room was in a worse state, most of the furniture from the entire apartment had been dragged into the small room and piled against the door in a makeshift barricade, though it had long since been torn down. The wasted bodies of two women lay strewn on the floor, dried blood staining the floorboards underneath them

"What happened here?" I whispered, my hand hovering over my mouth.

Cesar glanced to the two dead women, as if noticing them for the first time, then to the destroyed barricade by the door. He nudged an upturned couch with his foot.

"Looks like it didn't hold." he mumbled, shrugging his shoulders.

"Who would do this?" I said, looking away from the two women and their shattered skulls, my stomach heaving.

Cesar looked at me as if I were simple.

"Who you think? The other people in here, maybe those three in the living room, who knows. You just keep you eyes open understand."

I nodded, blinking away tears as I thought of the terror these poor women had gone through, and of their families outside the zone, who would never know the fate of their daughter, or mother.

"Hey, friend" Cesar whispered, flashing his torch across my face to get my attention.

I looked away from the bodies and into Cesar eyes — they were hard, his jaw firm.

"Don't think about it, understand? You don't think about any of it or you're done."

I looked back to the dead women, shaking my head "Cesar, this is … " my voice cracked.

"Move!", he barked, nodding to the door. I stole one last glance at the bodies then complied, my jaw set as we moved back out through the living room. The group we had passed sitting on the floor were no longer there. Cesar pushed me in the back.

"Keep moving."

We met Omar and Mateo in the hallway. Omar shook his head and lead a pale Mateo into the next apartment, the scuff of boot the only sound of their passing. Whatever horrors they came across on their search they kept to themselves, as did Cesar and I.

The search went on, room by room, as it had in four buildings previous, as it would in any others that showed signs of life until we found her. How long we searched I couldn't tell, the circle of light from my torch became my world entire, my breath and thumping heart a steady backdrop as we moved through the warren. Most people fled before us, some begged for help. To my shame I pushed them from me, violently at times, as did Cesar.

The poor people screamed and tumbled into the dark.

By the time we finally reached the top floor I was cold and covered in sweat; I had long since emptied my stomach, though still I wretched bile onto the stained floorboards at my feet.

Cesar turned and shone his torch on me "Maybe you better sit down or something?"

I took a small drink of water, most of it splashed down my front as I tried to steady my hands.

"I'm fine, keep going."

He waved me after him and disappeared into the last apartment as I fumbled to put the water back into my backpack. A flicker of movement to my right caught my eye and I froze, peering into the shadows at the end of the hall; for a moment forgetting that I had a torch.

The light came to rest on a mans back barely five meters from me. The jeans and singlet he wore hung from a skeletal frame, ribs and spine protruded through the thin material.

His chest heaved, as if he was having a severe asthma attack.

"Cesar," I whispered, glancing to the doorway, "Cesar."

I took a step towards the man, then another, holding a picture of Anna before me, "I'm looking for my wife?"

The breathing stopped. It was then I noticed the blood covering his hands and dripping to the floor at his feet. I stepped backwards, my breath froze as he turned. Blood covered his face, much of his skin was gone, torn away, along with one of his eyes. The other stared madly through me, seeing far beyond anything in this world.

I tried to call to Cesar again; fear robbed me of words and action. All I managed was to take a step back before the man screamed and began digging out his remaining eye.

14.

Cesar pulled my to my feet by the arm, his torch blinding me.

"Jesus be quiet! I told you to stay behind me. What you scream for?"

He scanned the hallway for any danger. It was empty save for a smear of blood on the floor where the man had been.

Omar and Mateo tore out of the apartment opposite, their weapons raised and ready to fire.

"There was a man, he was right there," I gasped, my body trembled with adrenalin.

"Scab spooked him," Cesar mumbled to the others, moving down the hall and checking round the corner, "you sure friend?"

I shook my head, breathing deep to calm myself, "Yes I'm sure. There was something wrong with him, his face, he'd torn his face."

Cesar stalked back to stand in front of me, his torch back in my eyes, "There's something wrong with all of them friend. You think we're carrying guns for fun? I told you to stay behind me."

His voice was low and laced with warning.

I pushed his torch away and pulled my backpack over my shoulder "I was right behind you Cesar."

He held my gaze for a few seconds, then sent the others on their way with a nod of his shaved head. They moved off into the next apartment, whispering amongst themselves and glancing back at us as we stood face to face in the hallway.

Cesar waved to the next doorway, his face like stone "After you friend"

I looked one last time to the pool of blood on the floor and followed him in, closing my mind to all but Anna, and to finding her before it was too late.

· · ·

Mateo and I sat against a graffiti covered wall and looked on as Omar and Cesar conferred quietly in Spanish. The sun was high in the sky, blazing down on the silent street before us. The heat was tolerable in the shade — the sunlight itself, and the radiation within it, was not.

Omar waved to the boarded up building across the road, then nodded back down the street, towards the wall. Both he and Cesar were beginning to raise their voices, though the source of their contention was beyond me.

"He says there's a hundred in there, maybe a little more," Mateo whispered. He was sure to check that neither of the cousins saw him translating.

"So why aren't we going in?" I asked, pushing myself to my feet, eyes glued to the small, three-story building. It looked identical to the two on either side, save for a gleaming metal cage surrounding the front door, and a serial number sprayed above it in black paint.

Mateo shrugged, lighting a cigarette and peering down the empty street behind us, "This place is fucked."

I followed his gaze, barely noticing the corpses scattered down the street. Weeds grew through cracks in the bitumen and hung from walls, crows sat sated and full — the zone an ever replenishing banquet.

"This is taking too long, she cant be here" I whispered, looking far beyond the burned out cars and rotting bodies to my Anna. "She cant be here."

Mateo spat to the street and offered me a smoke, which I waved away, looking to Cesar and Omar as they continued their debate. They spoke for another moment then parted. Cesar shook his head and stomped back to us, taking the cigarette from Mateo and drawing deep. Judging by the scowl on his face the negotiations had not gone as he had wished.

"This ones no good, army's got it locked down, we'll go to the next one," he mumbled, flicking the rest of the cigarette away with barely contained anger.

I grabbed his arm as he went to move off, turning him to face me "What the hell do you mean locked down? There's people in there, Anna could be in there."

He shook me off immediately and shoved me in the chest with shocking strength. He might have struck me had not Mateo intervened, stepping between us and speaking rapidly in Spanish. Whatever he said was enough to calm the murder in his uncles eyes, though veins still throbbed on his ink scarred temple.

Omar walked past, oblivious to the confrontation, the chatter in his earpiece constant. He started scanning the next building and mumbled in Spanish to Cesar— I stepped in front of him, my face inches from his.

"No, you speak to me. You speak English from now on."

He lifted his eyepiece and sat it on the top of his head, looking as if he hadn't noticed me before. A scowl wrinkled his pockmarked face and he turned to Cesar.

"Don't look at him, I'm the one talking to you. She's my wife, I'm paying you, and we're not leaving until we've checked, you understand?"

Omar's dark eyes narrowed, knuckles whitened around the assault riffle. We stood eye to eye for a few seconds before he spoke, his accent heavy.

"You see the gate over the door? We don't have the code."

"So get the fucking code" I roared. My voice echoed down the street, sending Mateo cringing and rats scuttling for cover.

Cesar intervened, pressing his cousin back a few steps "I told you he wouldn't leave it. So we get the code, like I fucking said eh."

Omar brushed Cesar's hand away and stalked a few paces, shaking his head and pointing to the building, his face flashing scarlet.

"I told you that's army business, we go in there things get bad for us. There's plenty more places to look. Why risk it when we don't know if she's in there? We search more, if nothing then we come back."

I looked back to the building, silent and dilapidated, a tattered curtain hung limp from a third story window. There was something about the building I couldn't ignore, something pulling me to it. Perhaps it was simply a desperate attempt to gain control over events, or just pure stubbornness, I'll never know.

"No, we're looking here," I said, my tone left no room for argument.

A few moments passed while Omar looked from me to Cesar, seeking escape.

"This is a bad idea, going in there could ruin everything. We're not ready yet," he said to Cesar.

What he meant by it I didn't know, nor did I care to.

"Fuck it," Cesar remarked with a shrug, "We're close enough, time this shit ended anyway, we cant wait forever."

Both cousins locked eyes for a moment. Whatever passed between them seemed enough to tip the scales in my favor, and when Omar next spoke his tone was no longer defiant.

"It'll take some time, maybe we have to pay someone big money for the code."

I crossed my arms.

"Do it, we'll wait."

• • •

I sat with Mateo while Omar paced back and forth, negotiating with his accomplice on the wall, and then another beyond. Cesar snoozed behind us, waving away a cloud of bloated flies that re-settled on his face as soon as his hand fell to his side.

"Man I hope you're right, I want out of this shit-hole," Mateo said, glancing to the boarded up building looming opposite. In the hour Omar had so far spent trying to get the code for the gates the temperature had soared, the silent building shimmered in the heat.

Doubt had already begun to twist my stomach while we waited, and I changed the subject quickly, motioning to Omar; still locked in negotiations that were quickly becoming more heated.

"How long have he and Cesar been coming in here?" I asked, watching Cesar's cousin stalk back and forth, oblivious to the sun beating down him.

"A year, maybe more. Cesar paid some big cash to get Omar transferred to the wall. He was in Iran before this."

I shook my head and looked away, remembering the angry rants Anna and I had shared at the governments insatiable appetite for foreign conquests, masked as humanitarian intervention. Those countries still possessed of natural resources and freedom must shudder at our impending benevolence.

"I don't understand why anyone would join in the first place."

"Huh?"

"The army. I don't understand why anyone would join, not after Taiwan. You'd have to be stupid to fight for a government that would abandoned thousands of men to the Chinese like that."

Mateo looked at me as if I were simple, his brow furrowed in confusion "What do mean join? He got conscripted, along with everyone else in his year at school when he was seventeen."

"Conscripted?"

"When the A.P.C's came and rounded them all up at school! You telling me you don't know?" He looked incredulous, as if I might be playing some bizarre joke on him.

I shook my head, my bewilderment too genuine for even the most skeptical to miss. He scowled and waved a hand at me, the simple gesture dismissing me as ignorant and beyond educating.

"It doesn't matter, that was before, they couldn't do that shit now. Things are different, we're trained now, the slums are ready if they try it."

He took another gulp from the bottle and passed it to me. The water was warm, and tasted of fluoride and plastic — Anna would have a fit if she knew I was drinking from a petroleum based bottle.

Omar raised his voice and gestured wildly, as if whoever he spoke to could see him. Sweat beaded on his pockmarked skin and soaked through his kaki uniform.

"They just came and took him?" I whispered, still disbelieving.

"Him and about three thousand others, all on the same day. It happened in the slums all over the country. The schools shut down after that, no one would send their kids. Cesar got some of the teachers to set up classes anyway, made sure we could all read and shit. They guarded us so they couldn't take us away."

Cesar waved at the flies again, shifting his weight and mumbling in his sleep — it was hard to imagine he, and those like him, taking such action.

"Cesar did that?" I asked, my voice incredulous.

He scowled and shrugged "Who else would?"

I glanced at Omar again, hand to his ear, rifle hanging from his shoulder. The negotiations had settle down somewhat; he no longer gesticulated wildly as he spoke, his pacing losing some of its fury.

Every minute that went by was unbearable for me, and I struggled to remain calm, knowing I would only delay results should I intervene. I waved a hand in exasperation and shook my head again.

"Why the hell does he stay then? Surely he could just leave now he's back home."

Mateo shrugged, swatting a fly from his mouth "Cesar wants him where he is. A lot of them died in Iran, others in Taiwan. Fucking government didn't want any of them making it back, but Cesar's getting them, one at a time. They're training us you know, and getting us more weapons. We're in every city, we're going to pull this shit apart."

"Quiet boy" Cesar sat up and glared at his nephew, a scowl contorting his face, "keep your mouth shut."

"Cesar, people don't know. I didn't know, about any of it" I said, looking at the gang leader with new found respect.

He snatched the water from his cringing nephew, drinking deep and throwing the empty bottle to the side.

"You don't know much friend."

· · ·

An hour later we had the code. Another ten thousand would be paid to a second accomplice now working for us beyond the wall, somewhere within the vast military network now spread throughout the world.

Cesar, Mateo and I, watched from the corner of the next building as Omar typed in the code on the metal gates and swung them open. Steel screeching on steel sent Mateo ducking, and the crows scattering.

We held our breath as Omar chambered a round in his rifle and reached forward, opening the wooden door with one hand and stepping back down the stairs, rifle raised to fire. Whatever he saw inside had him frozen for a moment. He lowered his weapon and waved us after him as he slowly walked back up the stairs and disappeared through the open door.

15.

I followed Cesar inside, the three of us turning on our torches. We left our masks off; the all pervasive smell of death was strangely absent as we moved into the foyer, black and white checks under foot. The stairs to the first floor and walkway beyond were packed with people, all of them shying from the bright light.

"Jesus!" Cesar gasped, crossing his chest, his cousin and nephew did the same.

Women, more than a hundred, filled the foyer, stairwell, and first floor balcony overlooking the front door. Many whimpered and shuffled away from us, shielding their eyes from our torches. From what I could see most were in good health, though their eyes were red rimmed and swollen. Many were crying softly.

"Anna!" I screamed, pushing past the others and mounting the stairs. Cesar tried to pull me back, but I would not be stopped. He swore and followed me up, calling Mateo and Omar after him.

"Anna!"

Some of the women whimpered and retreated further into the building, others simply huddled together with their arms about one another, faces turned from the torchlight.

I held the photo aloft and shone the torch so they could see "My wife, I'm looking for my wife, has anyone seen this women. Her name's Anna, have you seen her?"

I moved through the women, showing the photo to each and watching their faces closely. Cesar came behind and did likewise, though his appearance and aggressive manner frightened the women. Most could barely look at the bright light, their eyes were too inflamed. Others simply huddled in terror and refused to raise their heads when I approached them.

I was moving so quickly through the women that I barely noticed when a girl, no more than twenty, squinted at the photo. Her gaze lingered a second longer than the others before I lost her in the crowd. I scrambled after her, pushing screaming women to the side until I found her sitting against the wall, hugging herself. Her blonde hair was thinning, her clothes filthy.

I pushed through the last few women separating us and squatted in front of her, holding the photo close. "You've seen her haven't you? You've seen Anna"

"What she saying? She seen her?" Cesar yelled, moving through the terrified women to stand over us. The girl cringed at his voice and I had to stop her crawling into the shadows while a raised hand silenced Cesar.

When she refused to look up I lifted her chin and looked into her watery blue eyes. "I wont hurt you, you're safe now."

She looked over my shoulder to Cesar, then back to me. Her eyes pleaded for help, though she still seemed too frightened to speak.

"Where did you see her?" I whispered, there was only the two of us, nothing else existed.

She stammered for a moment as tears streamed down her face, her bottom lip quivered. When she spoke it was in a small, trembling voice, "She was here, she helped me before they took her."

She broke, sobbing into her hands. I caught a glimpse of a fresh bar code on her wrist.

"Who took her?" I asked, my voice barely a whisper. When she hadn't answered I shook her by the shoulders and asked again, though I somehow kept my voice soft.

She raised her head and looked to Omar, his rifle held at the ready, army chatter in his earpiece just discernable.

All eyes turned to him.

He shrugged, shaking his head to profess his ignorance of the actions of his peers. I turned back to girl and lifted her face to mine again.

"Where did they take her? Where?"

She shook her head and began crying again. I pulled her to me and held her as she wept; little more than a child, frightened and abandoned to die alone in the dark. Omar and I locked eyes, while Cesar murmured in his ear for a few moments. He finally conceded with a hand held to his temple, his eyes on the ground.

"Ok, I find out. I need to go back to the wall, we need to go. Leave her, you cant help them, they're all marked."

I nodded and hugged the girl tighter, "I'm sorry. I'm so sorry."

Mateo had to pry her from me. She begged for me to take her, to stay with her, for death rather than to be abandoned — we left her crying in the dark with the others.

Omar locked the gates behind us.

By the time we returned to the safe house we had ceased to speak, each avoiding the eyes of the other. My shirt was still wet with her tears when I lay on the bed, my back to the others and little left of my soul.

· · ·

"You know we're all stars, that's what we'll be when we're dead."

Anna lay on her back, gazing up through the overhanging leaves to the azure sky beyond. I put my wine down and lent over her, the remains of our lunch was spread over the blanket on platters.

"Like famous people?"

She rolled her eyes, "I'm serious, I think its amazing, that that's what we were, and will be again. This life is a dream, everything around us is just a blink."

"I don't know about that, this feels pretty real" I ran a finger down her neck, she wouldn't be goaded.

"Think about it, we spend billions of years as dust floating in space, as suns and planets, and we'll spend billions of years like that again. That's our real state, I think it's amazing. Makes death beautiful, like going back to what you truly are."

I leaned over and filled her glass, handing it to her as she propped some pillows under her head. I was happy to see her thinking about anything other than work. We hadn't taken a day off in months, the crisp Autumn day had been too perfect, the park opposite the apartment too beautiful to ignore.

"So what's all this then?" I asked, waving to the world around us.

She sipped the grape juice and lay back, eyes sparkling in the dappled sunlight.

"It's all dream, a dream of the universe. Maybe the universe is sentient. Maybe when this is all done, when we're all dead and the earth is gone, it might have learned something, grown somehow, that's why all this happens."

I finished my glass of wine, the fifth I'd had "So it doesn't matter what we do, one thing no better than the other. It's just one big experience?"

She thought on that for a moment, biting the inside of her bottom lip, "No, I think it's the opposite. If the universe is as big as we think, then no one thing can be greater than the other. Either nothing matters, or every single little thing does."

I awoke from a troubled, fitful half-sleep to Cesar and Omar drinking at the table, their voices low.

Mateo slept on the couch opposite, an empty bowl on the floor, the remains of a packet of potato chips scattered around him. Asleep, with his mouth open and arm as a pillow, he looked more the nineteen-year-old boy the tattoos and scars were intended to mask.

That I had let myself come so close to sleep when Anna was still out there alarmed me, and I immediately began rifling through my bag. For a moment I panicked, until I found the small bottle of stimulants in my coat pocket. I took twice the recommended dose of the red pills and pushed myself to my feet, swaying for a moment as the room span.

Cesar pushed a chair out when I approached and slid the bottle of whiskey across the small table, which I ignored. An awkward silence fell over the two cousins, neither of them looked me in the eye as I stood over them.

"Where is she?"

Cesar exhaled deeply and lent back in his chair, hands locked behind head "We found out where they've been taking women, lucky for you it's in the Zone friend."

I stepped back as if slapped, goose bumps prickling my skin "Why the hell didn't you wake me up? Why the fuck are you sitting here drinking!"

He held a hand to still my rising anger and waved me to take a seat "Settle down friend, there's still another few hours of dark. And there's something we need to work out first. Sit down."

I did as he bid, struggling to calm myself and sitting slowly, my eyes darting from one face to another. Mateo roused himself from the couch and wandered over to stand behind me, drinking a bottle of water and crunching the rest of his chips.

"So speak, what the hell is it?" I said, my leg began jiggling up and down — the stimulants worked fast.

"You tell him," Cesar nodded to his cousin across the table and light a cigarette

Omar shifted in his seat and cleared his throat, the normally quiet man uncomfortable having the attentions of the three of us upon him. He spoke slowly, his aversion to speech forcing him to punch out his words in a heavy accent. "Army's been collecting women and putting them in those buildings, then transferring them to another facility."

I nodded for him to continue, my face devoid of emotion, though my hands slowly balled to fists under the table.

He glanced to Cesar then continued, "I couldn't find out why they're doing it, but I know where they take the women, and I can get the security codes."

I'll kill them for touching you, I'll kill them, I swear it.

"So get the codes" I said, my jaw tight. Anger, the very same that would have seen me strangle orange hair to death so long ago in our apartment, welled inside me. I took a deep breath and stopped my jiggling leg with a supreme effort.

Omar glanced to Cesar again, who rested his thick arms on the table and mumbled around his cigarette "It's a little more complicated than that friend. The place they take the women is a secure facility. We figured out a way to get in there, but if we do this, the shits going to be heavy — we'd have to get out of here real fast and never come back, Omar as well. And that's no good, because we still have business in here. You need to pay us more."

I stood from the table, my voice low and trembling with barely controlled rage, "We had a deal Cesar, we agreed on an amount, I wont be fucking blackmailed by you, or anyone. You're going to help me find her for the amount we agreed on. This time you actually have to do what you've promised."

He scowled and stubbed out his smoke on the table "What you talking about?"

"You think I'm an idiot Cesar? You say people pay you to come in here and deliver food or medicine to their loved ones? Tell me, how do you actually do that when you have no idea how to locate a person? We've been floundering around in here for two days. Now you want more money to do what we already agreed on."

"Careful friend."

I leaned forward over the table, a murderous rage taking hold, spurred on by the stimulants surging through me.

"You prey on people, Cesar. You take their money and do nothing. Do you even come in here at all? Or just tell them it's done, that their mother or father, or child, have been taken care of? Meanwhile the poor people die alone, curled up in the dark somewhere, or get their heads caved in by some lunatic."

Cesar leapt to his feet, his chair crashing to the floor. Mateo and Omar scrambled away from the impending confrontation. When he spoke his voice shook with a fury that matched mine.

"You think you're the only person in the world who's lost someone? My brother was too far gone when I found him rubbing some dead woman's blood on his face, and I did him a mercy by finishing him quick, so you don't talk to me like that friend, ever! What the hell have you ever done that's bigger than you? You and yours just live your little lives out there like a bunch of fucking ants. As long as nothing touches you, you don't lift a finger. Well that's about to change."

Omar hissed a warning, but Cesar would not be silenced. A manic, half crazed look had filled his eyes, and I took a step back, despite my anger.

"You fucking people think its the Chinese or Arabs that want to destroy your country and turn you into slaves. It's already been done and you slept through it. You've been beaten by your own fucked government and none of you are doing shit about it. You're a bunch of brainwashed sheep. The cameras Omar and I have hidden around the Zone are going to stream to every fucking plasma in the country. And we'll bring down the blocks on the net as well. What do you thinks going to happen when this country sees what's being done to it's people? Or when the world sees the footage we've collected of mass graves in Iran and Syria, with our pretty white soldier boys laughing and pissing on the bodies? Or of women and children being burned out of their houses in Korea?"

I stepped back, fearing he might launch at me, such was the fury emanating from him. Gone was the violent, petty criminal I had taken him for. The man standing in front of me was something else entirely, something infinitely more dangerous.

"And when it starts to crack out there, we're going to pull the entire country to pieces. This shit stops, and my people are going to be the ones to stop it. For that we need money, lots of it to pay off stupid, greedy pricks who cant see past the tattoos on our skin and the dollar signs in their eyes."

I looked to Omar and Mateo, their dark eyes bored into me, their faces set in grim determination. In that moment I realized just how blinded I had been, first by apathy when my life was mine, and then by desperation when I'd lost her. I saw again the warehouse full of weapons in the slums and gang members packing them to be shipped off around the country. What Cesar thought would emerge from the anarchy he hoped to unleash was beyond my understanding.

I sat heavily, my eyes distant "You're insane," I whispered.

He leaned over the table, his face close to mine. "Maybe so friend. But that doesn't change where we are, and what needs to be done. I still want to help you. You think I need to do this shit? I'm doing this because I was too late for my brother, and if I can pull one person out of this sorry fucking hell in here and get paid for it I will."

He lowered his voice, eyes locked on mine. "So you better make up your mind friend. You want some people to die so you can have your lady back?"

I nodded, shock leaving me capable of little else.

"Then you pay me more."

. . .

A shaft of sunlight illuminated Mateo's hand, tattoos writhing as he struck a match and drew flame to cigarette. He drew deep, then ejected the magazine from his Glock and ran a finger over the top bullet. The trembling in his hands slowly lessened; by the time he slid the magazine into the weapon and chambered a round it had gone completely. He glanced to his uncle and Omar. The cousins sat playing cards on the stairs to our right, seemingly without a care for what would soon be done.

"Your lady must be something pretty special for all this huh?" Mateo whispered, barely glancing up from the weapon in his hands.

I looked to the photo I held and said nothing, running one of my fingers lightly across her face. The day we had accosted an old woman to take the quick snap of us seemed an impossible reality. I wondered if life could ever be that light again.

"Is that for her?" Mateo asked, waving the gun to the small bag at my side.

I spoke without looking up from the photo, "Her things; clothes, food, some medicine."

He nodded, then looked to the void above, and the women hiding on the first floor of the building, "Wonder what they're doing with them?"

"What?"

"All the women, what do think they're doing?" he said, his face took on a slightly animated sheen.

"I … I don't know. I'm trying not to think about it."

He missed the hint and continued, narrowing his eyes conspiratorially "Probably using them for some kind of experiment or something. Maybe the army gave it to them on the outside so they'd get put in here, you know? Cesar says it must come from the government, because we cant find anyone bringing that shit in. Never heard of anyone making it or selling it either. And why would people take it anyway? Everyone knows it kills you."

I looked away, hoping he would change the subject.

"You've seen the raids on the news right? The buildings being burnt down, dealers with their faces covered, being arrested? Cesar says it bullshit, all fake. I never met anyone in the pen says they had anything to do with it. It's the government that's got all these people addicted to it."

"Jesus I don't give a shit, it's irrelevant!" I snapped.

He jerked as if struck, picking up the silenced Glock and ejecting the magazine for the hundredth time, "Fuck man I was just talking. I thought you would have been all over that shit to figure out why your lady … I mean, you know, why people take it."

138

It was all I could do not to strike him. My hands balled into fists, my voice tightened. I took a deep breath, "I told you she didn't take it. My wife isn't one of these people. This whole thing is a mistake. You'll see that when we find her."

The conversation ceased, an awkward silence taking hold. I looked to the piles of crates in the corner, empty food and water containers lay scattered on the chequered floor. Likely the food deliveries weren't as frequent as needed, the provisions were probably consumed in a near riot as the hundred or so women tried to take enough to stay alive.

Mateo ejected the chambered round again and inspected the bullet, his hands were beginning to tremble again, the colour draining from his face once more.

"You don't have to do it Mateo. It should be me," I whispered, looking to the closed doors. He light another cigarette and went back to fussing over the gun, smoke billowing through beams of sunlight to disappear into the void above.

"It's cool, I can kill these army fucks no problem," he lied. He sounded an unconvincing mimic of his uncle. His shaking hands and downcast eyes betrayed his bravado.

I raised my voice and looked over to the cousins on the stairs "Cesar, I'm doing it, not Mateo"

Cesar replied without looking up from the game "Not you're decision friend. The boy needs to earn his marks, and I'm not risking something happening to you — you cant pay me if you're dead."

"I have earned them" Mateo protested, standing with the gun at his side.

"Not to me you haven't, not until I've seen it with my own eyes boy," Cesar said. He slammed down what must have been a winning card, to Omar's dismay.

"If he doesn't want to he doesn't have to Cesar." I challenged. I heard muffled voices and movement above, the women perhaps frightened by my raised voice.

Cesar swore under his breath and looked to his cards one last time before he threw them down and stormed over. His nephew cringed as he snatched the gun from him.

"Stop fucking about boy. A man with your marks fears nothing, never hesitates, so you better not."

Mateo nodded, head hung and face ashen.

"And you," Cesar turned to me "you're keeping out of the way like we planned, understand? And when it's done you move quick."

I pushed myself to my feet, eyes locked with his "What if they're faster, more ready than you think? What if they're supposed to radio back?"

"What ifs can get you killed friend. There's a time to stop asking and pull the trigger, like when I saved your ass out there."

I looked away, a hand going to the scab on my lip — put there by the three young men who had beaten me in the slums.

"That's right friend, if I'd hesitated instead of following you out of the slums those little pricks would have beaten you to death and taken your car."

"They didn't have to die," I murmured. For a moment I was in the past, waking to the roar of automatic gunfire and hot blood spraying across my face. I stumbled to my feet in time to see Cesar and two other gang members laughing as they threw the corpses of the young men to the side of the road.

He stepped closer, face inches from mine "There are times you have to make a move and take what you can from the world, before it does the same to you, and if you don't pull it off then too bad. Now's one of those times friend."

"Quiet!" Omar hissed. He stood from the stairs with his head cocked to the side. A moment later we all heard it, an engine distant but fast approaching.

"Up the stairs, you don't come out until its over," Cesar warned. He and Mateo squatted in the shadows by the door.

Omar ran past, flicking the safety on his rifle and waving me up the stairs "Go, move, now!"

I did as he bid, there was little else I could do. I tripped once going up the stairs — the army uniform and boots I was wearing were a few sizes too big.

Enough beams of sunlight streamed through the cracks in the boarded windows to illuminate the foyer below, my hiding place like some opera box seat. The floor began to vibrate as the engine came nearer, my heart thumped in my chest.

I watched Cesar put a hand on Mateo's shoulder, and whisper to his young nephew. The boy nodded, face pale, pistol gripped in both hands.

The vehicle pulled up outside, the engine idled for another thirty seconds before rumbling to a stop. Two doors opened then slammed shut. Footsteps on the stairs, a code being punched into the keypad on the gate.

I whispered a prayer, my hands balled to fists as the hinges on the metal cage screeched.

The front door opened, spilling sunlight into the foyer and blinding me for a moment. I opened my eyes to see two soldiers walk in, weapons slung casually over their shoulders, their manner relaxed. A third man, wearing rubber gloves and plain green overalls followed them; a large silver medical kit by his side.

Mateo and Cesar rose from the shadows behind them.

16.

"I'd fight a dragon for you."

"Huh?" Anna looked up from knitting her scarf; her year-long project at last coming to an end.

I stretched out on the couch and rested the book I'd been reading on my chest. "Like the guy in this book, I'd fight a dragon for you."

She rolled her eyes, scowling as she picked at a knot "I'd settle for doing the dishes more."

"I think my one's a little more impressive. Are you even watching this?" I asked, looking to the television opposite. The hero was having a hard time of it, the aliens he battled seemed to have little fear of his grenade launcher. The situation looked hopeless- he'd have to pick his game up if he was going to save the half-naked woman cowering behind him.

Anna glanced to the screen then back to the knot she battled "That's the problem with men, you're all so preoccupied with grand gestures. Life's right here in front of you and you're all waiting to wrestle a bear."

"We just want our ladies to know we'd do anything for them, that's all" I said, nudging her with my foot.

"But you wont do anything. You'll fight a dragon but you wont tell a woman you love her. You'll go off to war or get drunk and hit someone, but not change a diaper. If you guys really want to show us you love us then just be there for us when it matters."

"Like fighting a dragon to save you," I murmured, crawling along the couch and resting my head on her lap. The move interrupted her battle with the tangled wool. She rolled her eyes and dropped the mess of blue material onto my face.

It was over in seconds. Six loud pops echoed throughout the foyer, along with the men's strangled screams. Then silence, broken only by the sound of one the soldiers crawling across the floor, gurgling blood and gasping for breath. Cesar shoved his pale nephew towards the struggling man, yelling in Spanish until the boy fired twice into the cringing soldiers back.

Mateo looked up from the dead man and locked eyes with mine for a moment. Thankfully for him his uncle didn't see what I did before he wiped a hand across his face and pushed the smoking Glock into his jeans. Cesar's plan depended on speed above all else, and I pushed thoughts of the dead men from my mind as I ran down the stairs, taking them two at a time.

Omar raced outside to the A.P.C to check for other soldiers, while Cesar handed his nephew a heavy knife, almost a cleaver, and watched as he cut off the right hand of each man; the boy retched as he hacked away, blood splattering his face. I looked on as stone, my heart hard and jaw clenched. I would have watched it done to a hundred such men if it led me to my Anna.

He put the three hands in a garbage bag and handed the bloody blade back to his uncle. Cesar scowled and berated the boy as he wiped the blade clean on one of the dead men, then ushered him outside and into the open personnel carrier.

When Omar came back inside he froze for a moment, gaze fixed on the mutilated bodies of his dead peers. Whatever he felt at seeing the men killed he kept to himself, rousing himself to action and waving me outside.

"Hurry! Rapido!"

I was careful not to look at the dead men's faces as I passed, though my foot slid in their blood.

The door to the building we left open.

Cesar and Mateo were already sitting in the back of the personnel carrier reloading their weapons, surrounded by enough equipment to fit out a small hospital. Two beds sat along either side, heavy restraining straps for both hands and feet testament the vehicles sickening purpose. Mateo threw the garbage bag to me as I slammed the doors shut, sealing the two tattooed gang members out of sight.

The engine roared to life, and the vehicle began pulling away before I'd closed the door. I was breathing heavily, adrenalin coursed through my body, sharpening my senses but leaving my stomach nauseous. We were beyond the point of return, success or failure to be decided in the next twenty minutes.

* * *

The streets of the Zone whirred by. Omar pushed the heavy armoured vehicle to its limits, the tyres screeching on every corner.

"You know what to do when we get there?" he asked, his tone slightly manic. Sweat trickled down his cheek. It was the first time I'd seen any hint of fear or doubt in the man.

I nodded and let out a lung full of air.

He glanced across to me, "Just move quick, but confident. If anyone's looking at a camera every second counts, understand?"

I nodded again, and tightened my grip on the garbage bag of bloody hands.

We slowed down as we neared the cinema, our destination halfway down the block; hidden from view on the top level of a car park. Omar whispered a quick prayer and turned off the street, manoeuvring the wide vehicle through the abandoned cars that were scattered about on each level. He drove slowly, both of us keeping our hats pulled low to obscure our faces from any cameras that might be watching.

When we turned up the last ramp I thought we were undone — metal gates loomed before us. We slowed and looked to each other in a panic until they rattled open. Omar let out a deep breath and drove through slowly, unsure of which way to turn until I caught a glimpse of a cluster of low, steel demountable units to our right.

He turned and accelerated quickly, glancing to me as we neared the buildings, "Ready?"

My eyes were fixed on the armoured demountables looming ahead, seeing through them to my Anna, and the life we would live when we were together again.

"Ready."

A steady beep sounded as we backed into the loading bay. Surveillance cameras watched our every move. Omar got out as soon as he pulled the vehicle to a stop, keeping his head down and face hidden from the cameras poised atop the loading bay. I followed him with the garbage bag held behind my back.

I fished one of the hands out and passed it to Omar. He swore and wiped the blood covering the index finger on his shirt before pressing it into the reader. The keypad lit up, a ten second countdown initiating as he punched in the code. I prayed under my breath the thirty thousand dollars paid to his contact had been well spent.

The keypad flashed green and the doors slide open with a hiss, an empty steel passageway stopping at another set of doors a few metres in. I returned to the personnel carrier and unlocked the back door, but did not open it. I stood with my back to the security cameras, sweat trickling down my spine.

Please god, please.

Omar repeated the same ritual to open the second set of doors. I waited until I heard the keypad accept the code, then flung the door open. Cesar and Mateo, tattooed demons both of them, burst from the vehicle and raced inside, their guns raised to fire.

I followed them in and sealed the doors behind me.

· · ·

The rapid popping of Omar's silenced assault rifle echoed down the hall as I ran to catch up with the others. I arrived to see Cesar reef a cowering young man to his feet and throw him to a sealed door as Omar typed a code into the keypad beside it. A jarring beep and flash of red had him swearing and kicking the heavy steel doors — screaming death to those on the other side.

Two men in lab coats were bent over a bank of computers to the right of the doors, their bodies torn and bloody.

"What the hell happened?" I yelled, adrenalin pumped though me, so much that I shook.

"Open it!" Cesar roared, shoving his pistol into the young mans cheek and pushing his face into the blinking keypad. He was perhaps only a few years older than Mateo, and terrified.

"Please, don't kill me," he wailed. His eyes were closed, as if he expected a bullet at any moment.

"You don't want to die then you open this fucking door!" Cesar roared, grabbing his hand and pressing it to the keypad.

The boy typed in a code, and sobbed when the keypad flashed red, "It's locked from the other side, I cant."

"Fuck!" Cesar screamed, striking him across the face with the butt of his pistol. The boy fell to his knees clutching his shattered face, blood seeping between his fingers.

Mateo stood over him with his gun pointed at the top of his head, and though his hand trembled I knew he would pull the trigger if needed. All eyes were glued to the door as Omar pulled a small cylinder from his belt and sprayed a man sized circle, the gel hissing as it ate through steel.

"How long?" Cesar growled, pacing back and forth.

"A minute, maybe less," his cousin replied. He stepped back from the door and loaded a fresh magazine into his rifle.

"Have they called it in?" Cesar asked, looking to the bullet riddled computer equipment. Blood pooled under the two dead men, neither of whom looked to have had time to move, let alone call for help, before they had been killed.

Omar held a hand to his ear and listened to the chatter of the army on the wall and beyond. He shook his head "Nothing yet, we're good. Hit it hard," he nodded to the still smoking door. Light could be seen through small holes here and there, I heard muffled voices on the other side.

Two heavy kicks from Cesar and the steel fell into the next room with a crash that shook the floor. The cousins stormed through the still sizzling hole and opened fire at a target out of my line of sight, though I heard whoever it was scream for mercy a second before it was denied them.

I arrived in time to see two more men in lab coats crumple to the floor — blood covered the wall behind them.

"Jesus!" Cesar gasped, crossing his chest. Omar did likewise. The cousins lowered their weapons and stared about in shock.

I pushed past them and stumbled down the long room, picking my way through countless women strapped to stainless steel operating tables. Their skin was flecked with scabs, thin tubes snaking from their wrists and stomachs. A hundred machines hummed, screens above each woman displayed images and data beyond my understanding.

Cesar said something to me, though his voice was distant, as was Mateo's. They could have been firing their weapons and still I wouldn't have noticed.

Nothing else existed as I lent down and pulled Anna to me.

17.

"God I love that smell, what is it?"

"Shampoo," Anna laughed, flicking her long dark hair across my face and darting from my reach. I soon caught her, and we weaved through the crowded sidewalk with our arms around one another. The late night air was thick with red powder. The dust storm had come after weeks of sweltering weather, though now a cold front had rolled in, sending everyone rummaging for their coats once again. The lights of the city glowed as though shrouded in fog, giving it an almost cosy ambience.

I breathed deep of her hair, for a moment I was somewhere else, somewhere beautiful; Anna a flower in a wasteland

"Mine never smells this good" I murmured.

"That's because you hardly wash it, and when you do it's with the cheap stuff."

"Well we peasants cant afford to live as you do, your majesty."

I hugged her tighter and squeezed through a silent crowd, their eyes glued to an overhanging plasma. The results from the latest vote had fallen in line with government recommendations, as they always did.

"God, look at them. They really believe it don't they?" Anna mused, glancing back at the concerned huddle.

I shrugged, looking ahead to a massive flashing billboard. The poll results were quickly replaced by a benign doctor administering care to a smiling patient. The number to call when reporting the addicted scrolled over the peaceful scene.

"It's not their fault, look at this shit, there's no escaping it," I mumbled with a wave of my hand to the city around us.

"You don't see us huddled around listening to it," Anna contested.

The screens changed back to writhing flesh and catchy beats, the multitude disbanding and carrying on their way.

That's because we're smarter than everyone else," I mumbled. My eyes remained glued to the screen, "much smarter."

A light tap on the cheek brought me back. Anna's face flashed dark, though a smile touched the corners of her mouth, "Like the lyrics do you?"

I cleared my throat, "how else am I going to learn how to 'treat my ho nasty'?"

Another tap on the cheek and rolled eyes rewarded my cleverness. I followed demurely as she lead me another block, stealing glimpses at the screen whenever she wasn't looking and resisting when she tried to drag me into the packed second hand clothing store.

"I cant, it's too much for me in there. I'll guard the door."

"I was going to try on a few more things."

"You said we were just picking up the jacket," I whined.

Eyes rolled as she let my hand go and pointed to the nearest screen, the next single more lurid than the last. "I think you'll be fine," she said, pecking me on the lips, "wont be long"

"Wait!" I pulled her back up the stairs and ignored her protests as I buried my face in her hair and breathed deep, only letting her go after a few seconds of bliss.

"Time to move friend."

I opened my eyes. The hum of computers and steady beep of twenty or more heart monitors filled the room. Cesar and Mateo stood on the other side of the table, faces ashen as they watched me stroke Anna's angular face. The young man Cesar had struck cringed by their feet, cradling his bloody face.

Since I had lost her this moment had played through my mind. Always Anna had thrown herself, weeping, into my arms.

My deluded fantasy crumbled as I called to her again and still she would not wake. Small scabs and lesions were showing on her pale skin, her once glossy hair lank and thin. I kissed her and buried my face in her hair, whispering for her only while I squeezed her hand, begging her to wake, to come back to me. I might have stayed there forever had Mateo not pulled me to my feet.

"Come on man, we have to get her out of here. We have to go."

I shook him off and opened the small bag I had brought. Tears blurred my vision as I began unpacking her clothes; blind and deaf to all but my Anna.

"What the hell you doing?" Cesar asked.

I laid out a pair of jeans and a black Led Zeplin shirt; bought for a small fortune from an old man who'd kept it for over sixty years, a gift from his father.

"Hey, friend, no time for that shit, we have to move, now" Cesar implored.

I continued fussing over her, oblivious to all.

Cesar swore under his breath and reefed the young man to his feet, shoving him towards Anna. "Wake her up, unhook all the shit. Do it quick and I might not kill you."

The boy began to cry, his legs barely able to hold him as he disconnected the various machines surrounding her. Blood caked the side of his head where Cesar had struck him, flattening his curly hair to his scalp. I stood back from laying out the contents of the bag and watched him pull needles from her arms and sensors from both her temple and stomach. Blood welled from her veins and I put pressure on the wounds until they where bandaged. In my haste I used the Led Zeplin shirt to wipe some of the blood away, ruining the faded print. I swore and began cleaning it with the last of my drinking water.

Cesar snatched the shirt from my hands and threw it to the side, "Fucking wake up! Look where you are, we need to move, now!" he roared, grabbing me by the shoulder and turning me to face the twenty other women lying strapped to tables.

I nodded manically and unscrewed the bottle of stimulants, tipping two into my hand. Cesar knocked them from my hands with a roar "Enough of that shit, they've fucked your brain. We're leaving, now!"

After weeks of little food and less sleep I was weak, my limbs frail and barely up to the task as I tried to pick my Anna up and carry her.

"Put her down, you," Cesar shoved the bleeding man towards Anna as I lay her back down, "wake her up, now. Give her some adrenalin or something."

The boy began to sob quietly, blood dribbling from his mouth to the floor. One of his eyes had swollen shut, the other was wide with fear.

"I said wake her up!" Cesar roared, cuffing him on the back of the head. The blow sent him stumbling forward — if not for the table Anna lay on he would have tumbled to the floor.

"I cant," he wailed, cringing as Cesar stalked towards him and pressed a gun to the boys cheek.

"You get her up now boy or you'll wish we shot you with the others, understand."

"I told you I cant, she's been sedated, all of them have. I cant wake her."

He turned to me, his one working eye pleading for mercy "Please, this isn't my fault, I just collate data and prep patients. I can give you the serum, the one we give the women in the buildings. I can help you."

I looked into Anna's serene face. Her chest moved up and down in a steady rhythm — for all the world she looked caught in a peaceful sleep.

"I can help you," he repeated, a trace of hope had crept into his voice, and he took a step closer to me.

"This serum, it can save her?" I murmured. He glanced to the clenched fist at my side and nodded.

"I want all of it, now."

He grasped at the lifeline, scurrying across the room and pulling a metal case from a small refrigerator. He opened the lid to reveal over fifty vials of clear liquid.

"She only needs one a day, there's enough to stall the virus for another three months. I can do it for you, just don't kill me please, I'll look after her for you."

He must have noted my confusion. I looked to Cesar and Mateo, their expressions a mirror of mine.

When I looked back to the boy his one eye had widened in disbelief, and for one brief moment fear seemed to have fled him. "Jesus, you ... you don't know do you?"

"Know what?" I asked, a confused scowl contorting my face.

He looked to the two gang members, guns still in their hands, dark eyes upon him "I thought that's what this was, I thought you all knew."

His jacket tore as I screamed and pulled him to me, rage turning my world red. "Know what you fucking son of a bitch? These people have an addiction and you treat them like animals. You tell me what you're doing to my wife, fucking tell me!"

One hand squeezed his throat, the other balled into a fist and raised to strike; he gasped for breath, and barely managed to choke out his next words.

"None of the people in here took any drug. There is no drug, there never was."

18.

My fist hovered for a moment, his words freezing me in place until my hand slipped from his throat and he stumbled backwards, leaning on a bench and gasping for air.

"It doesn't matter anyway, we cant stop it, we're all going to die soon, everyone's going to die," he wheezed.

Still we were silent, eyes darting to one another. Cesar shrugged his shoulders and shook his head slightly.

"The fucking virus! We don't know where it came from. It's speeding up and we can't stop it"

"Stop talking shit you little bastard!" Cesar stalked towards him with his gun raised to strike. The boy cringed, a hand shielding his face.

"Jesus, just open your eyes, everyone's infected, everyone. Why do you think the shots for the Monkey Flu and Ebola were mandatory?" he wailed.

Cesar paused, brows knotted incredulously. He and I shared a look of complete bewilderment.

"We were treating the virus. It's been going on for five years and it's getting worse, we're all going to die."

He sat heavily and begged us to spare his life, though if what he had told us was true, then that was far beyond our power.

． ． ．

"Be careful, gentle," I fretted, hovering over Anna as Mateo and Ashley, the young scientist, lowered the stretcher to the mattress in the safe house. Sweat poured from them, their limbs trembled with fatigue. I pulled the cloth covering Anna's face away. She slept soundly, oblivious to being carried at a jog for nearly ten blocks in high uv.

The armored vehicle we had to leave behind at Omar's insistence, the tracking systems built into them were too difficult to deactivate in the little time we had.

The cousins collapsed at the table, throwing weapons to the side and stripping their soaked shirts off. They drank half a bottle of water each, the rest they poured over their heads. Cesar gasped and shook droplets about the room like a dog after a bath and slapped Omar on the shoulder, congratulating his pensive cousin.

Mateo joined them and the three relatives went through four more bottles of water before Whiskey became the drink of choice. Even the normally somber Omar allowed himself a small smile. The three of them seemed oblivious to what we had just learned, seeming to not care that they might well be infected with the same virus as those wandering the streets outside. Perhaps to men like them, death was something they faced and even expected every day. Learning they might die sometime in the not too distant future would hold little fear for them, either that or success had temporarily robbed them of their senses.

I squatted by Anna's side and watched Ashley check her vital signs before he inserted a saline drip into her arm; blood still caked his hand from the wound on the side of his head.

"She'll need two of these a day. There's ten here, you can buy more from any pharmacy," he explained.

"When will she wake up?"

He ignored my question and looked to the others, his face pale, lips blistered from the sun. His eyes were glued to the half empty bottle of water in Mateo's hand.

"Mateo, water," I barked.

Ashley caught the tossed bottle in both hands and sucked it dry in seconds, leaning against the wall with his eyes closed.

"When will she wake up?"

"Jesus I need more," he gasped.

"When will my wife wake up you son of a bitch!" I roared, knocking the empty bottle from his hand and grabbing him by the shirt.

"She can't wake up. I told you the serum has a sedative in it, if you miss a shot the virus will accelerate. Once that happens you cant stop it, she'll die."

I looked back to Anna, the only hint she lived was the steady rise and fall of her chest. To have her so close and still not hear her voice, or look into her eyes was a torment beyond endurance. I was desperate for her to know I was here, that I came for her and that she was safe.

"Can she hear me?"

He shook his head, looking to the ground at his feet.

"This serum, show me how it's done."

He nodded manically and reached for the metal case he had brought, a loud hiss sounding as he opened the lid. Waves of nitrous fog cleared to reveal row upon row of small vials filled with transparent liquid.

"She needs one a day. No more or you could kill her; the sedative is very powerful — it's designed to put the patients into a deep torpor, one that keeps their organs functioning and little else," he said, loading one of the vials into the insulin pen and pressing it to her arm.

"She's already had one today. When you do give her one, just press it to her skin and pull the trigger, at ten each morning."

His voice was drowned out by Cesar roaring with laughter behind us. We both looked to the gang members on the other side of the room, lost in their own world as they celebrated victory with boasts and drink around the table. Cesar slapped his nephew on the shoulder and congratulated him on his killings, which spurred the boy on to brandish the wound he had cut into his arm a lifetime ago during the party at his mothers. He bragged of the new tattoo he would embellish the scar with. Cesar and Omar both critiqued his proposed choice. Their celebration was quickly gaining momentum, the bottle of Whiskey fast disappearing.

I tried to pull Ashley's attention back to Anna, but his eyes remained glued to Cesar as he began reloading one of his Glocks.

My temper flared and I grabbed him by the shirt, "I'm the one you need to worry about boy. You're alive because of me. This clinic better be what you say it is, because if I take her to the other side of the country and find out you lied I swear to god I'll kill you."

"I'm not lying, they've had a breakthrough, they can help her," he stammered.

"And they'll take her? I just show up with the money?" I said, letting him go and looking back to Anna, anger melting from me as quickly as it had come.

"They'll take anyone who can pay. Dr Lomac, one of the men you killed, had been emailing them. If you mention him they'll accept her."

"And they can cure her?" I asked. Anna's hand was in mine, my eyes glued to her face. Though she had lost a lot of weight and her skin was pallid and scab flecked, she was still beautiful, she was still my Anna.

A second later everyone ducked, eyes to the ceiling as two choppers thumped overhead. Plaster crumbled from the walls as they passed. Omar put his earpiece back in and leapt to his feet while the rest of us looked on with breath held.

"That for us?" Cesar asked, in a low voice. His eyes darted to the locked metal plate sealing us in the safe house — his hand hovered over the assault rifle on the table.

Omar waved him to silence and stalked to the other side of the room, the tension in the room became palpable until he shook his head "It's nothing, food drop near the convention center. If they do know it's not on any channel I'm getting."

Cesar spat to the side and snatched the bottle of whiskey from Mateo. His cousin and nephew joined him in another drink, though their previous merriment evaporated. They spoke quietly amongst themselves and glanced over to the two of us hovering over Anna.

"She going to be alright?" Cesar asked, his tongue was already heavy, though still he gulped from the bottle.

Ashley nodded, but kept his eyes to the floor.

Cesar spat to the side again and turned to me, "You taking her to that place he told you about in the mountains huh? It's a long way friend, maybe you get caught on the road."

The warning in his voice could not be missed.

"What I do once we're out of here is my business Cesar. We wont get caught."

He lent back, holding my gaze as he lit a cigarette and passed the box to Omar. "What if he's lying, about all of it?"

Ashley, his fear momentarily forgotten, raised his head in his defense "I'm not lying. They can help her there, maybe even the baby."

For a moment his words escaped me, and I simply nodded and looked back to Anna — within seconds my mind could no longer shield itself from their meaning. I heard Cesar swear under his breath and whisper to the others, but still I stood, my fist trembling at my side.

"Why was my wife in there with those other women?" I whispered.

Ashley started to sob, and shrank from me, as if he might somehow escape my notice, "It's not my fault, I didn't do any of it."

Cesar yelled a threat from across the room, and when the boy next spoke, his words, though small and distant, shook the world.

"She's pregnant, all of the women in the lab were."

19.

"We'd be good parents," Anna mused. The scent of the bolognaise she stirred wafted through the apartment. I focused on grating the cheese and ignored her comment, hoping that would be the end of it.

"We would you know," she pressed.

We locked eyes for a brief moment before I cleared my throat and put the cheese back in the refrigerator.

"Being good at it isn't reason enough."

"Well they'd be good looking too, from my side, and permits are still easy enough to get," she smiled and ground some pepper to the pot.

"Yeah, maybe. Maybe they'll be pricks."

"Don't, please don't," she pleaded. She stopped stirring the pot and looked away.

"What? How do you know?" I asked, leaning on the edge of the table and crossing my arms.

"I just do," her voice caught.

"No one knows. If people could get it right then why the hell are there so many fuck ups out there? And having your genes checked to get a permit is a fucking insult; the means test and physiological profiling were far enough."

She was silent.

"Everything's perfect with just the two of us. You really want to ruin the next eighteen years for some teenager who'll turn around and throw all our hard work in our faces? How many times have you seen it? The parents give everything and then the kids just piss it all away."

She was close to tears by now, as she always was when I contested starting a family. "They'll be our kids Riley, they wouldn't be your enemies. Why cant we just let go for once and stop pretending we're so different to everyone else? You'd be a great dad."

I was already shaking my head "You don't know that. You don't know I wont turn out like my father. You want to live with some violent, drunken bastard?"

"Riley you barely drink, you're a saint, stop using your father as an excuse. Why don't you just admit you're scared" she sobbed.

"I'm not talking about this bullshit anymore."

We splashed through the dark sewers, the water sloshing to our knees black and foul. Mateo and I carried Anna on the stretcher. I was struggling after nearly an hour of following Cesar through the sewers. My will alone pushed my legs to follow one another, my hands to grip the sweat covered handles.

No one spoke, exhaustion left us little energy to spare. The only sound echoing through the dank tunnels was sloshing water and our heavy breaths.

Ashley walked beside us and monitored Anna. He was now a willing captive, his faith in my promise of life greater than his trust of the government, and what would happen to him should he be found; the sole survivor of a compromised operation. Whether he identified me or any of the others to the authorities was irrelevant; I was a wanted man regardless, three dead intervention officers my death sentence should I be caught.

As for Omar, Cesar had decided the risk was too great for him to return to the wall. His contacts would likely be uncovered, and it would not take long for them to name him. He was now a fugitive, though such a fate was always going to be his, death or flight the only possible ends to his enforced servitude.

We pushed on through the dark, losing our footing now and then. Ashley steadied the stretcher until we regained our feet. He and Mateo worked in shifts — I would allow no one to relieve me. She was my wife, my Anna, and I would carry her to the ends of the earth if needs be.

My legs were faltering, my grip slipping, by the time we finally felt the wind on our faces and staggered out into an overgrown storm water canal. The moon shone full in a clear sky, Anna's skin pale in the moonlight.

I collapsed by the outlet pipe while the others moved with speed and discipline. Both Mateo and Omar stood guard with ready weapons while Cesar radioed his people. I brushed a piece of cobweb from Anna's cheek and sat transfixed, my eyes never leaving her face, nor my hand hers.

Two cars roared towards us along the canal with the headlights turned off. Each of the Mercedes was occupied by armed gang members who got out and stood watch as we piled in.

Cesar and Omar got in the lead car; Mateo, Anna and I followed in the second. Radios on the dash were alive with the chatter of Cesar's people keeping watch in the night and monitoring security frequencies.

The men drove at breakneck speed, the petrol engines roaring in the narrow canal. I cradled Anna in my arms and held her tight as we weaved through piles of rubble and burnt out cars, the tires screeching on slime covered cement.

Soon we burst out onto a tar road running parallel to the highway and the drivers flicked the headlights on. Moments later we tore up the onramp and merged with the never-ending stream of traffic moving along the freeway. The city stretched from horizon to horizon on both sides, an endless matrix of light that robbed the sky of stars.

Ashley, sat cringing in the front between Cesar's people. I had grave doubts Cesar would honor my promise of life to the boy after I left the city, but there was little I could do, what energy remained I needed for Anna. I absolved myself of all responsibility for his fate.

"Hey, hey doctor boy," Mateo nudged the back of the seat to get Ashley's attention, though his dark eyes remained glued to the window, and the hive of millions beyond. "Is that shit you said about the virus true?"

"Yes," Ashley whispered with his head hung, wedged between two demons in the front of the car.

"And we all have it, everyone?" Mateo pressed.

He nodded, his voice small and defeated "Everyone."

We drove in silence from then on, and for the first time in nearly two weeks I slept soundly, with Anna's head on my chest and my hand cradling her stomach.

• • •

I was awoken by searing light and Mateo nudging my leg with his foot. I covered my eyes with my hand, my mind swimming as I struggled to comprehend what was happening.

He shoved me again, this time with more force, "We're doing it now. You have to hurry."

I sat up, still shielding my eyes until they adjusted to the glare of the flickering fluorescent above the bed. The thick scent of mould brought the reality of the run-down hotel on the edge of the slums crashing in upon me.

The voices of Cesar's men washed through the open door of the small bedroom; voices and the sound of weapons being loaded.

Anna lay beside me, as she had when I'd finally succumbed to sleep after hours of sitting by her side watching her chest rise and fall. I spent a few moments fussing over her until Cesar yelled through the doorway.

"Get up friend, we're going now."

There was a temporary lull in the men's conversation outside, then the sound of bullets clicking into magazines and hushed conversations resumed. I rubbed a hand over the thick stubble covering my jaw and swung my legs over the side of the squeaking bed, nodding to myself. I ignored all but the sound of my breath as I blew out long and deep, my eyes staring vacant across the room.

One more push, just a little more and she's safe.

I squeezed her hand and stood, squinting as I emerged into the living room. At least ten of Cesar's men crowded the small space, all of them armed and wearing Kevlar vests. They looked at me with dilated pupils, their faces expressionless under scars and tattoos.

The moment passed and they returned to their preparations, their actions rapid and focused — I noted the empty boxes of army-issue reflex enhancers and stimulants on the coffee table.

Cesar and Omar pushed through the milling men, coming from the kitchen, where Cesar had no doubt been fortifying himself with Whiskey — he was the only one not wearing body amour. Instead he was dressed in his usual dirty white singlet, a Glock strapped across his chest.

"Timo and Hector are staying here to watch your lady," he said, waving a thick arm to the only two men not busying themselves with preparations. They leaned against the wall near the front door, their facial tattoos, more than their features, were now familiar to me. The two men had been at the gang-owned hotel since we had arrived two days ago, standing watch over me at Cesar's orders, and no doubt making sure I wouldn't disappear without paying him.

I looked around the room, my stomach knotting as I watched the men prepare for what looked like a serious confrontation; all of them had night vision equipment resting on top of their heads, and grenades clipped to their vests.

"Cesar … this is too much. I can get this done by myself, or with Mateo."

He dismissed me with a wave of his hand and called his nephew over. He began adjusting the straps on the boys vest, "I told you make it tight."

Mateo reddened with embarrassment and endured the heckles of the other men with a tight smile until Cesar rubbed him on the head and shoved him towards the front door. The rest of the men took it as their signal to move out, all of them slinging weapons over their shoulders and filing into the hallway outside. Cesar issued a few last minute instructions to Timo and Hector. The two men tested their earpieces and nodded.

"Cesar!" I said, stepping in front of him and blocking the doorway — he looked at as he'd almost forgotten who I was.

"Cesar, this is stupid, it's not necessary," my voice was steady, yet already what should have been a command sounded more of a plea.

He scowled and grabbed me by the shoulder, ushering me out of the small hotel room. Omar followed and closed the door behind us.

The men waited at the end of the hall, muttering amongst themselves and re-checking their equipment. Cesar sent them onwards with a wave on his hand.

"It wouldn't have been necessary, if you hadn't killed three steadfast agents, along with your friend. They don't let shit like that slide — ever. You should have told me before the zone, it changes everything."

He shoved me down the hall towards the waiting men.

My skin prickled, a wave of nausea turning my stomach. "It was an accident, I didn't mean ..."

He cut me off, walking past me down the hall, "What you mean in life doesn't matter friend; only what you do. Now hurry up, this ends tonight."

. . .

Omar drove the Mercedes, Cesar in the passenger seat beside him. They spoke quietly in Spanish. Both were tense and alert, their eyes scanning the dark streets for any hint of danger. Mateo and the other young gang member sitting next to me did likewise, their fingers curled around the triggers of small, compact machine guns resting on their laps.

The car smelled of cigarettes, sweat and gun oil.

Now and then we passed a cab or garbage truck. Other than that the streets were near deserted, as I assumed they always were in a residential area at 3am; the quiet served only to heighten the tension.

I glanced behind us to the second carload of Cesar's men following. Even when the dark green BMW passed under the harsh street lights the tinted windows concealed the men from the world. I shuddered to think what might happen if the police attempted to pull either vehicle over.

Omar pulled the Mercedes to the curb and switched the lights off. No one spoke as the second car rumbled past and parked further down the street. The neighbourhood was deserted, a slight breeze stirring the trees in the park. Five men, all of them wearing night vision equipment and carrying the same compact machine guns as Mateo, got out of the other BMW and melted into the park.

We waited a few moments until they radioed back that all was quiet. Cesar, still cautious, strapped a night vision eyepiece on and looked across the road to the dark apartment blocks, mumbling to Omar as he adjusted focus.

He spoke to me without turning, "the whole building normally blacked out like that, friend?"

I followed his gaze to our apartment complex, my stomach knotting, though there seemed nothing out of place to warrant it. The entire complex had an impressive energy rating, kept that way by mandatory regulation of electricity. No one would risk going over their allowance by leaving lights on at this hour if they didn't have to.

"It's an E4 area, that's why it's so dark. There's some security lights that come on when you get near the doors."

Cesar smirked, "They even tell you when you can have your lights on huh?"

I looked back to the blacked out building, and to the others on either side. I hadn't thought of it that way.

He and Omar shared a few words before Cesar issued a command to the man sitting beside me. The gang member shed his weapons and got out, throwing a coat over his shoulders to conceal his Kevlar vest. He walked down the road and crossed the street half way down the block. A few moments later he reappeared as the security lights flicked on outside the apartment. He carried on down the sidewalk and crossed the road when out of the light, returning to the car at a jog.

He spoke briefly with Cesar through the open window, shrugging his shoulders and shaking his head. Omar waved to Mateo, who strapped night vision equipment on and got out, taking the mans weapon with him.

They both moved off into the park and were quickly swallowed by the dark.

"Nice neighbourhood," Cesar remarked, looking around at the well maintained grounds and comfortable apartments opposite. He continued speaking, though still he didn't look at me

"You know friend, the more luxury you have in life, the more suffering you cause in the world, and the further removed you are from it."

When I hadn't answered he turned to me, the scars and tattoos covering his flesh making a demon out of the man underneath.

"You know that don't you? That this shit isn't the reality of the world. You people are going to learn what life really is."

Why it mattered to him what I thought was beyond me. I nodded and looked away, trying not to think of the life Anna and I had shared here. There would be no going back for us, the past was another world, lived as a dream; I cared little for what became of it.

We waited while Omar spoke into his radio to the men from the other car. I imagined them somewhere in the park, creeping through the dark and scanning the shadows for danger. The deep sense of foreboding that had taken root in the pit of my stomach continued to grow. Fear and doubt gnawed away at me, no matter how convincing the security measures being taken by Cesar and his people.

"Maybe we should come back another time, something feels off," I said, peering into the shadows around us.

Cesar shook his head and got out of the car, "I've waited long enough, this needs to be done. Bring the shovels."

I cast one more glance across the road to the silent apartments before I grabbed the two shovels at my feet. Mateo and his partner emerged from the dark and joined us. I led Cesar and his cousin through the park, avoiding the paths and lights where I could. We moved deeper into the more heavily wooded side of the ten acre expanse of manicured gardens, kept green at great cost to those who could afford to live in our district.

Omar constantly murmured into his headset to the five men from the other car. I never saw them, but it was clear they were moving ahead and to the side of us. Cesar and his people operated with military efficiency, and I wondered if any of the men guarding us were part of the stolen generation Mateo had told me of in the zone — either that or they'd been trained by them.

I scrambled up a small rise and crawled under some bushes, followed by Cesar, Omar and Mateo. The other man stood guard at the bottom. The small clearing under the dying oak was as I'd left it, and I swept aside the rotten log and leaves so carefully placed a week ago.

The shovel bit easily into the loose soil underneath.

Mateo slung his weapon over his shoulder and picked up the second shovel; by the time we hit the two watertight backpacks we were waist deep in the hole, a mound of earth encircling us. Cesar and Omar smoked and chatted quietly while they watched us work, confident in the protection afforded by the men spread throughout the park.

"Jesus, you put them deep enough?" Cesar mumbled, flicking his cigarette to the side and slapping his nephew on the back as the boy scrambled from the hole.

"Too many stimulants," I mumbled, handing the first bag out to Mateo and reaching down for the second.

The act likely saved my life.

Automatic gunfire rent the night, bullets thudded into the earth around me and whirred overhead. I panicked and foolishly tried to scrambled out of the hole, until blood sprayed across my face and the bag I had handed Mateo landed on top of me. I fell backwards, taking what cover I could as more guns than I could count began firing in both directions across the park.

I buried my face to the earth and awaited the bullet that would surely kill me. Men screamed in English and Spanish, more bullets whirred overhead and struck the earth encircling the hole. I heard men running close by, then more gunfire. Hot shells sprayed into the hole and burned my skin. I curled tighter into a ball and prepared for the end.

The sound of heavy vehicles came roaring across the park, then bullets striking metal. A moment later a deafening explosion rolled through the night.

The sound shook me from my stupor.

I threw both bags from the hole and scrambled out after them, crawling over a pair of legs as I went — Mateo lay with his face in the earth, blood seeping from the back of his head. His one visible eye looked far beyond anything in this life, and I froze in shock, unable to look away until more bullets threw earth into my face and instinct sent me scrambling away.

Everywhere I looked the white flash of automatic weapons lit up the night. Another explosion had me covering my head and burying my face into the earth as clods of dirt rained down around me.

I caught a glimpse of two armoured vehicles coming to a stop at the base of the hill and disgorging a score of heavily armed police. Two of them fell immediately, the rest sheltered behind the vehicles as Cesar's men fired upon them from across the park.

I crawled along the ground towards the thick trunk of the oak, dragging the bags as I went. Omar sat with his back to the tree, a hand pressed to a gushing wound in his neck. He seemed not to see me until I shook him and tried to drag him after me — he was heavy, and I wouldn't get far with him. He pushed me off with a hiss and handed me a pistol. A moment later he fell to the side and dropped his hand from the wound.

A better man might have stayed and tried to stop the bleeding, or taken the gun and joined the fight against the police now moving up the hill. Perhaps I should have tried to find Cesar, the man who had done so much to bring my Anna back to me.

I did none of those things.

I pushed myself to my feet and ran, taking the two bags of money and gun with me.

Branches whipped my face and tore skin, but still I ran, the sounds of battle receding behind me. Every moment I expected a bullet to tear into my back, or police to storm from the shadows and bear me to the ground. The thought of Anna lying alone in the hotel drove me beyond exhaustion, beyond the limits my malnourished body should have allowed.

By the time I tore across the road and into an alley the rapid gunfire had lessoned to sporadic shots, muffled and distant. I ducked behind a dumpster as two personnel carriers roared past and turned into the park. A helicopter thumped somewhere out of sight.

I stumbled on, my lungs fire, the bags of money like lead. I ran another three blocks until I found a cab. The tyres screeched as I jumped out into the middle of the road with a handful of money held above my head. I threw myself across the back seat, my body trembling, muscles burning.

I closed the door seconds before a chopper roared overhead and search lights illuminated the cab. Both I and the old driver froze, our breath held. My heart thumped in my ears until the light moved down the street.

The driver let out a lung full of air and turned to me, a frown adding more lines to a face already deeply etched. A lifetime of hardship and loss could be seen in his faded, blue eyes.

"What the hell did you do?"

"What any husband should," I whispered.

He held my gaze for a few moments more and nodded. We pulled away quickly, and said nothing more to one another.

. . .

I changed cabs twice, the last one dropped me off a block from the hotel. The two men Cesar had left to watch over Anna were gone, a scattering of cigarette butts the only hint they had been there at all. My heart stopped for the few seconds it took me to cross the tattered living room and throw the bedroom door open. Anna lay serene and unmoving, and I allowed my self a brief moment of weakness, collapsing to her side and holding her close.

The few people that saw me carrying her through the dingy lobby and out to Bens old Ford said nothing. No one would question what went on in the gang owned building, no matter how nefarious it appeared.

I laid Anna on the back seat, covering her with a thin blanket and propping her head under a cushion. I was in shock, I began to shiver with cold, though I was covered in sweat. The magnitude of what had just happened — the deaths of Mateo and Omar, and likely Cesar as well, began to dawn on me, and I found myself squatting by the car with a shaking hand held to my mouth, my eyes staring into space.

Too many had died — Anna would never have wished it so.

I don't know how long I sat there, long enough for my knees to be aching by the time I was brought back to the world by distant sirens. I scrambled into the car and swallowed a handful of stimulants, tipping most of a bottle of water over my head and slapping my face.

"Don't worry babe. It'll be fine, I can do this," I mumbled as I started the car and pulled away from the hotel.

I took the roundabout route through the slums. It seemed the only area of the city devoid of roaring police choppers and personnel carriers. An eerie silence hung over the ruined streets. No cars moved, no young men loitered on street corners. Most houses were blacked out, the shutters drawn.

How we made it out of the city I'll never know, but we soon left it, and its forty million ghosts, behind. Hours later its sky glow still dominated the eastern horizon, and I prayed that would be the last I ever saw of it.

Before us stretched nothing but black night and empty highway, and the new life Anna and I would build together.

20.

We drove through the night, the sun rising blood-red behind us. A heat haze shimmered over the wasted landscape by the time it had cleared the horizon. Now and then we passed pockets of green, as some enterprising homestead used a deep water bore to stave off the inevitable. Such sights were a rarity, the majority of the land was an abandoned wasteland, perhaps irreversibly so.

Anna lay on the back seat, her dark hair covering the small pillow under her head. Here and there I could see her scalp, her skin pale and scab flecked. Such alarming signs of her condition drove me to push Bens car to its limits, and I prayed the old Ford had enough life left to see us to our destination.

I took stimulants every few hours. When they weren't enough I hung my head out the window. I knew I was destroying myself, that my mind and body might well be ruined, but it was a price I would pay a thousand times to bring Anna back.

Sometimes, when I could bare it no more, I pulled over and lay with her, stroking her hair.

"I'll fix this babe, we're leaving it all behind."

The toll booths and security checkpoints we passed through were automated and unmanned. The first time I used one of the false identities I had procured in the city I held my breath and prayed the twenty thousand dollars I'd paid to an acquaintance with business connections in China had not been wasted. The card was scanned and we passed through unchallenged. I used a different card at every checkpoint, lest suspicion be aroused by the many miles we traveled. I also cycled through three different sets of license plates, changing them before we came into sight of the camera riddled blockades.

A separated identity card saw fuel flow at automated refueling stations. The credits attached would be more than enough to see us to the clinic, and then out of the country.

Day blurred into night and night into day. Our journey took us across the country, through abandoned, drought-wasted flatlands and decaying towns — a prelude to the fate of all.

The military issue rations Cesar had given me were chewy and tasted of chemicals and cheap flavorings, but they kept me alive and that was all I needed. We rarely passed cars, the road quiet save for the occasional truck hurtling by.

At the second refueling station I checked and topped up the fluids in Bens old Ford. The leaks were getting worse and the motor hissed alarmingly every time we stopped. There was little I could do; the Mercedes Cesar had organized for me I had left at the park, the Ford had been my only choice.

I sat in the back while I waited for the radiator to cool and pressed a drip into Anna's arm, wincing as her blood filled the needle. I hung the bag of saline and nutrients from the roof and sat with her head on my lap, stroking her hair and whispering of all I would do to make things right for her, and our child.

The insulin pen let out a small hiss when I pressed it to her arm and pulled the trigger; the serum emptied into her immediately — her life, and the coma that robbed me of her, prolonged for another day.

I threw the empty vial away and fussed over her for another few minutes, rearranging her position and wrapping her again in the blanket before we left, the strip of dark mountains growing on the horizon our goal. Soon they towered before us, the city and its troubles lost to us forever on the other side of a ruined continent.

I took the last of the stimulants early on the third morning as we wound through arid foothills, then started the long climb up the eastern side of the mountains. The land disappeared behind in dust and haze.

"I don't believe it. People have always fantasized about some paradise in the west; its some kind of subconscious hangover from a thousand years ago or something," I argued.

Anna put her fork down and shrugged, sipping her glass of water, "I didn't say I believe it, it's just what people are saying, that's all. Things like that sometimes have a grain of truth. Maybe there are some areas that have been spared, improved even with the changing weather."

I swallowed a mouthful of lasagna and topped up my empty glass of wine. We were the last in the small restaurant, squeezing in a late dinner after work. "Maybe. It's hard to believe we all wouldn't know about it."

"How would we? The government controls the web, what's on TV, everything. All the refugees are told to come to the east, some of them are even forced! Everything's monitored because of Steadfast. It could be that just having the majority not knowing is enough"

Anna was getting that look in her eye, I tried to steer the conversation into less controversial territory.

"You think Ben can handle a Monday without us? It's only two weeks away." My mothers birthday was coming up, an all weekender Anna wanted Monday to recover from.

"You know he can, he's been up to it for over a year, just let go' old man. Anyway, who knows what's going on over there? Could be that the elite want to keep the masses away, keep us penned up in the East so we can all be controlled, and just a select few can enjoy the benefits of regular rain and fertile soil. Maybe there's things going on there they don't want us to know about."

I sighed "Sounds a bit big to cover up, seriously, there's no way something like that could be kept quite."

She glanced out the window to the thronging sidewalk, and the large blaring plasma across the road. "You don't have to keep something quiet to keep it a secret, you just have to make everything else loud."

As we crested the mountain and began our descent I noticed the difference in the air immediately; what had been hot and dry became cool and moist. The land around us became steadily greener as we drove down the western side of the range. What houses we passed were large and prosperous, high security fences topped with cameras protected their occupants from the world. Some of the opulent estates sat near the road, but for most the only hint that they existed were solid gates, and behind them, roads winding deep into the forest.

It was into one of these winding forest roads that the GPS led us. We drove for miles along the narrow dirt track, through towering firs and redwoods until I reached a small, unassuming steel gate, locked to a steel post with thick chain. I turned the engine off and stepped out, blinking to clear my vision and breathing deep of the crisp mountain air.

The forest was dark and quiet, night was close and the air was thick with the heady scent of the woods cooling after a long day in the sun. I stumbled to the gate, shaking my head and slapping my face to wake myself, and cursing my stupidity at not bringing enough stimulants. Fatigue was creeping in, weeks of scant food and little sleep threatening to break me.

I swore under my breath as I scanned the forest on the other side of the gate, seeking some way around. There was no intercom that I could see, no way of summoning anyone to let us pass. Indecision and exhaustion left me standing as if in a trance. My vision clouded for a few moments before I regained my senses and shook myself to action.

I returned to the car and tipped the last of my water over my head. I stuffed two protein bars into my jeans, along with the loaded Glock Omar had given me before he died.

Even now, after Anna had lost so much weight, I struggled to lift her — my body a ruin after weeks of deprivation. I held her to me regardless— if it was ten miles to the clinic I would see her there.

A mans voice cut through the deepening gloom.

"What are you doing?"

I spun to see a white van parked on the other side of the gate. Two men stood on either side dressed in white orderly uniforms, barely distinguishable in the deep shadows.

"I said what are you doing?" The man repeated. They walked slowly towards the gate, their manner guarded. As they neared me I saw that the man who spoke was the older of the two, gray touched his dark brown hair, while his face was deeply tanned and weathered. His thickly built younger companion walked slightly behind him, eyes darting from me to his older colleague.

They came to a halt on the other side of the locked gate. Neither one came to my aid, though I was clearly struggling to hold Anna. My mouth flapped a few times before words came, "Is this the clinic? My wife needs help, I was told to come here."

They looked to one another and then back to me, the older man gave me a quick up and down and glanced to the beaten up old Ford behind me.

"Password?"

I looked from one face to another as I thought on what to say next, "I'm colleague of Dr Lomac, my wife is one of his patients."

I prayed they knew of him, that Ashley had told the truth and that these men had not heard of his recent death.

Another look was thrown to the old car behind me, before he waved a dismissive hand, a scowl darkening his tanned face, "This is private property. You'll have to go back the way you came."

I readjusted Anna, pulling her higher and pressing her face into my neck. I took a step towards the men, my words and will iron.

"I'm not going anywhere, I've just driven across the country to get my wife here. I have the money, one hundred thousand in cash."

I noted the flicker in the man's eye, though still he made a show of mulling it over for a few seconds, "Wait here."

He walked back to the van and spoke quietly into a radio for a few moments, leaving his young, burley companion to wait nervously in front of me.

My arms were beginning to tremble, my back to ache. I pulled Anna up again, and breathed deep — I would not be able to hold her for much longer.

Grey hair returned a moment later, his feet crunching on the dirt road, "I need to see the money."

I nodded, relief flooding through me as I stumbled back to the car and lay Anna on the back seat. I opened the trunk and grabbed the bag I had prepared before leaving the city, passing it over the still locked gate to gray hair, who handed it to his younger colleague to count.

The mans eyes never left me.

"When was the last time you saw Dr Lomac?" I knew Anna's chance of being admitted, and her life, depended on my answer.

"I haven't seen him in months, but I spoke to him on the phone. He wouldn't tell me where he was, he mentioned the army."

"How do you know him? If you're not a member then you shouldn't know about this place."

I had no idea what he meant by member.

"We were colleagues once, when he heard my wife was sick he told me to bring her here. He said you would take her, he said from the data he'd been sharing with the clinic that you'd made a breakthrough."

I don't know how it came out so fluidly; I even believed it myself. The man nodded and walked back out of earshot and waited for the money to be counted. His young assistant whispered to him when he had finished. I noted the smile they shared — he had found the extra fifteen thousand.

When next he spoke his tone had lightened, the scowl that had creased his brow lessoned, though never quite left "We'll bring the van through, just stand aside please."

I did as he bid, my heart racing as the young man unlocked the heavy chain and pulled it from the gate. The electric engine couldn't be heard over the tires crushing through the gravel; it was easy to understand how I hadn't heard their approach.

The two men moved quickly and professionally, the back doors of the van opened to reveal a high tech interior of monitors and medicines, all surrounding a hospital bed a few feet off the floor.

They were about to pull it out when I told them not to bother. I lifted Anna from the back seat and carried her across to the van; I could have wept at how light she was. The young man helped me lay her on the gurney.

I fretted and tried not to get in the way as they busied themselves with checking her vital signs and hooking her up to some of the machines. I cringed as they pushed needles into her.

"What have you sedated her with?" The man asked.

"The serum Dr Lomac gave me, it's the one he's been working on, it has a sedative in it. Do you need it?"

He shook his head and returned his focus to Anna. One of the monitors summoned the younger man to the front; he returned a few moments later and whispered into his workmates ear.

Grey hairs ever-present scowl deepened, "Were you aware she's pregnant?"

"Is everything ok, is the baby ok," I asked. I began to panic immediately.

He shared a brief look with the young man, who nodded and looked away.

"Its fine, I'll make sure they're aware of it as soon as we get back," he said, pushing a drip into her arm. A moment later they climbed out and went to close the doors.

"Wait. I'll ride with her. I'll leave the car here," I put a foot on the back of the van to step in.

The man held a hand to my chest, "I thought you understood, we don't allow outsiders in. The clinic is for patients and staff only."

I froze with my foot still poised on the van, for a moment not comprehending what he had said.

"What? You cant expect me to just let you take her! I cant leave her." I said. My temper flared, violence flashed through my mind, sharp and brutal. Such impulses were becoming common, and I wondered what kind of atrocities our soldiers committed in foreign wars after weeks of stimulants and reflex enhancers. I took a deep breath to calm myself, lest I ruin Anna, and our child's, last chance.

The man sent his young helper to hold the gate open with a wave of his hand, "It's not up for negotiation. You're lucky we're even taking her at all, we're over capacity as it is. There's a town about ten miles from here, I suggest you go there and rest for awhile. Give me your contact details and we'll call you."

"I cant lose her again," my voice broke.

He snapped me out of my indecision "Look, this is the best place for her, you have my word,. You know what happens to sufferers out there when they're discovered. She'll be safe here, we can halt the virus permanently. You still have a choice, but I advise you to let us do our job."

Whether he had any real concern for Anna, or was simply making sure he could hold onto his money was unclear. He was right though, I had no other choice. I looked back to Anna, strapped into another bed with machines snaking from her body, the very thing I had sacrificed so much to free her from.

"I want a moment with her," I whispered.

He looked at his watch and nodded "Just a few minutes. The sooner we get her back the better."

They stood to the side and talked quietly while I climbed into the van and sat beside her. A heart monitor beeped steadily, tubes feed oxygen into her nose.

My voice caught when I first tried to speak, and I looked away for a moment to regain my composure.

"Anna, you have to go with them, they're going to help you. I wont be far away … I want you to know that no man ever had a better wife, and no child will have a more perfect mother. I'll be a different man than I was, I swear it."

The machines kept up their steady tempo around us and I held back tears as I stroked her face and kissed her.

A few moments later the van disappeared around a bend in the forest and I was alone, the only sound the hum of a thousand crickets now that night had come.

I stumbled back to the car and collapsed against the side, sinking to my knees and weeping like a child.

• • •

I pulled into a roadhouse on the outskirts of the town and was directed across the street to a small row of rooms attached to the side of a large, dilapidated house. The decrepit, purple haired women who answered the front door looked startled at having a stranger standing on her front porch; it took me a few moments to convince her that I was simply after a room, and not some wanderer in search of a hand out.

She prattled on about the sights to see in the surrounding mountains as she led me to my room, either not noticing the state I was in or not caring. She seemed oblivious to the world I came from, there was no mention of the weather or refugees, or foreign wars; normally the first topics of conversations in the city.

I thanked her and stuffed her hands with money, closing the door as she protested the large sum. I collapsed into the sagging mattress and lost consciousness before the bed had stopped squeaking.

21.

I spent the next three days sleeping, and when I wasn't sleeping I was eating at the roadhouse opposite the motel. I didn't go into the town proper, I had no desire to be surrounded by people whose lives were still their own. I could see no reason as to why people were being funneled into the eastern cities, nor did I broach the subject with the few people I spoke to. From all I had seen, this side of the country seemed fit to harbor millions. There had been no road blocks stopping me from traveling here, no warnings or threats to turn back. Anna had been right, people hear and see only what they are shown. We follow the path of least resistance, and that path led to the glittering cities of the east.

My cell never left my side, and I constantly checked for messages and missed calls. I was desperate to know how Anna's treatment had progressed, and knowing she was so close, and likely awake and waiting for me, was almost too much to bear.

By the second day, senses I had not known gone began to return to me. I no longer took stimulants, and as their effects faded it became clear that they were not only designed to stave off sleep and keep the sense sharp, but also to numb the mind of the effects of trauma. The reality of Bens death came crashing in upon me late on the second day.

I saw the bullet I'd fired tear his life from him again and again.

The bloody scene flashed through my mind every time I closed my eyes. That night I awoke covered in sweat, and for the briefest of moments I saw him lying on the small sofa opposite, his face covered in blood, just as I had left him.

I had no one with whom I could share my grief, or guilt; no one to consol me when I sat grinding a fist to my temple and mumbling like a lunatic, as if I could somehow erase what I had done.

I fell into despair and paranoia, and began to worry about my mother and brothers. I worried that in failing to capture me for the murder of their colleagues, the police might well be punishing those more easily reached. I thought on calling them, and came close to dialing my mothers number before I threw my cell to the side. Being contacted by me would only bring the attention of the authorities to my poor family, if they weren't already.

I spent hours sitting on the edge of the bed staring into space. Without Anna, I was alone in the world, my life ruined and barely worth living. Eventually sleep took me, I dreamt of blood and fear, and all the while the eyes of the dead followed me.

I awoke to a gunshot, the sound quickly morphing to the ringing of my cell. I glanced to the small clock by the bed — it was four thirty in the morning. I had locked out all numbers save for unknown ones — I knew before I answered that it would be the clinic.

"Mr. Dainon?"

"Yes, is this the clinic? Is Anna ok?" I asked in a near panic. I swung my legs over the edge of the bed and rubbed sleep from my eyes.

"Yes, your wife has responded very well to the procedure, you brought her to us just in time." His voice was deep, his manner polite.

I let out a lung full of air to calm myself, though still I began to shake with excitement.

The man continued, "I think it's time you left Mr. Dainon."

I leapt to my feet, rubbing a hand over my face and stretching my eyes, "What do you mean leave? I'm staying here until my wife's treatment is over, until I can pick her up. Who is this?"

I began pacing around the room.

Silence for a few moments.

"Mr. Dainon, you've been misinformed. Our patients must remain at the clinic indefinitely. Releasing them would pose too great a security risk."

I stopped pacing and took a breath to remain calm. My was mind still sluggish with sleep, and struggling, "Wait, just stop, who is this? What the hell are you saying, that she has to stay there forever?"

Adrenalin was beginning to fill me, my heart increasing its tempo.

"Not forever Mr. Dainon, but certainly until those in power come to their senses and inform the public about what's truly happening out there. Full democracy needs to be restored. Surely you understand the need for secrecy Mr. Dainon. We operate only because of the support of a select few in power — cooperation that would soon evaporate should knowledge of the clinic become general."

"Wait, just stop. You cant expect me to leave my wife and child in some strange hospital in the mountains until the government decides to topple itself. I'm coming to get them now. I want someone to be at the gate in twenty minutes."

Silence again.

"Hello, are you there? Hello."

When the man next spoke he stammered, his confidence faltering "I ... I'm sorry Mr. Dainon, I thought you had been told about the procedure by Dr Lomac ... about what would happen to your wife, and the fetus."

My heart stopped it's frantic beating, the world became silent "Told what?" I whispered.

He stammered again before he cleared his throat and regained some of his composure, "I'm sorry Mr. Dainon, your wife's pregnancy has been terminated."

The phone fell from my hand. The man continued, his voice small and distant, "Mr. Dainon? Mr. Dainon, are you still there?"

What was left of my mind tore through my skull.

. . .

The tires of the old Ford screeched as I burst out onto the road, turning towards the mountains, towards my Anna.

I pushed the car to its limits, and drove with little regard for any traffic that might be coming towards me on the dark mountain road. Within ten minutes I spun the car up the dirt track. The forest was a blur, dust billowed behind to swirl in the gray predawn as I tore around bends and rattled over the potholed road.

The chained gate loomed ahead — I pushed the pedal to the floor and braced myself. A jarring crash crumpled the front of the car and threw me into an exploding airbag with shocking force, but still I carried on. I thrashed away at the deflating airbag and pushed the rattling vehicle along the dirt road.

The engine was spluttering and grinding as I rounded a final bend and burst out of the forest into an area of rolling pasture. The road wound up a gentle slope to a large cluster of buildings on a rise. The main structure was a stately place, standing proud and affluent, flaunting its grand pillars and marble facade.

Another set of gates loomed at the top of the hill, this time of a more solid make than the one in the forest. I would stop for nothing, the faltering engine roared to life one last time and propelled over a ton of metal at close to sixty miles an hour.

The gates gave way instantly, the car passing as though a bullet through glass. My momentum carried me up the last thirty meters of paved driveway, and it was almost too late when I saw the large stone fountain looming ahead. I slammed the breaks and ripped the wheel left — the car struck the edge of the fountain and tipped on its side. I was thrown across to the passenger seat and into the door as glass shattered and the car ground to a halt at the steps leading up to the grand home.

I was cut and bloodied, ribs were likely broken, but I felt none of it as I scrambled to free myself of the wreckage. I heard people yelling and running towards me.

I climbed up towards the drivers-side window and tumbled down onto the gravel as two men in white orderly uniforms rounded the front of the car. They ran to my aid — and froze when I stumbled to my feet and raised Omar's gun.

"Get back, fucking get back! You come near me and I swear I'll kill you both," I screamed, backing them towards the stairs leading into the mansion. They held their hands high and walked backwards; I was limping badly and was having trouble lifting my right leg high enough to follow them up the stone steps.

The men were young and well built, and one of them, perhaps thinking I was bluffing, leapt at me when I stumbled. I pulled the trigger when he was still a few feet from me, the bullet struck him just below the hip and burst out his rear. He screamed and tumbled down the stairs, sprawling in the gravel and whimpering as he struggled to staunch the flow of blood with his hands.

He friend was of a more cautious nature, stretching his arms high above his pale face and backing through the large open doors.

Inside the manor, staff members milled around in confusion, their minds slow, sleep still lingering. Most were still dressed for bed, their eyes red and hair disheveled. The young orderly used his initiative and slowly dropped to the floor with his hands on his head. None of the others had the sense to follow.

I didn't know what I was going to do, and I simply followed the mans lead and ordered the rest to do likewise.

"Get on the floor, all of you," I roared.

They looked at me as if stunned animals, neither following my command or fleeing in terror. I roared and fired the gun into the ceiling, the sound was deafening — the crowd dove to the floor with military precision.

I glanced down the three brightly lit hallways that extended off from the entrance, each one held at least a dozen doors. I was beyond myself, panic and fear drove me, and I was ready to murder any who stood in my way.

I wiped a strand of bloody saliva from my torn lip and waved the gun over the huddled crowd "Where's my wife? Where's Anna Dainon? Tell me where she is or I'll start killing people, tell me!"

I was screaming like a lunatic, my entire being trembled with adrenalin, though endorphins numbed my senses and gave the whole scene a surreal, almost dreamlike quality. Through it all, an overwhelming, almost animal like instinct drove me to find Anna.

No one answered, rightly fearing that in doing so my attention would be upon them, and their death might soon follow. I reefed a cowering middle aged woman in a pink night robe to her feet, yanking her head back by her short-cropped blonde hair.

"Anna Dainon," I whispered.

When she didn't answer, perhaps out of shock, I pressed the muzzle of the gun to her cheek and pulled the hammer back.

"Where!" I roared.

Her bottom lip quivered and she looked close to fainting, though somehow she found the nerve to speak, "She's in D-block."

I took some pressure off the trigger, though still I pressed the muzzle of the gun into her cheek, and might have fired had she not answered my next question immediately.

"Where? Tell me where."

She pointed out the doors "Outside, to the left, past the solarium."

She closed her eyes and began weeping, perhaps expecting I would now kill her. I dropped her to the floor and stumbled out into the predawn light, the cowering people spread around the floor forgotten. The young man I had shot lay to the side of the path in a pool of blood. He cringed and lay still when I passed.

A broad expanse of well kept lawn stretched away from the main building under a dark sky tinged with dawn. I turned left and followed a cement path running along the side of the manor. I limped as fast as my injured leg would allow, a burning pain spreading through my chest. My mouth was slowly filling with blood, which I simply spat to the side. A dome-shaped building loomed ahead, light shone through its glass ceiling and out the large double doors hanging open at its front.

As I passed I saw beds radiating out from the center of the round building. Most of them were occupied, the patients all lay as if asleep, their heads shaved. A young orderly moved amongst the beds, nodding his head to the music he listened to through a small set of earphones.

He didn't see me, and I stumbled on, my mind numb to all but finding her, my focus complete. Once past the solarium the original main building ended, a newer, single story addition was joined to it at a right angle. I entered cautiously, with the gun held ready to fire.

Inside looked like a small hospital ward, with a nurses station sitting opposite the entrance. A few gurneys sat along the wall, an empty wheelchair by the door. There were no staff; I guessed they had been warned of my approach and had sensibly fled. I lowered the gun and limped down the long corridor bisecting the building. Doors were spaced evenly on either side, each with a small glass panel at head height, allowing me to see into the rooms as I passed.

What I saw knotted my stomach, a cold sweat forming over prickled skin.

The first room held a man sitting in a narrow bed, his eyes glazed and mouth open. His hair hung loose to his shoulders, a short beard, roughly trimmed, covered the bottom half of his face. I noted the date of the mans admission on the ledger hanging from the door — three years ago.

The only name was his first, followed by his patient number — John 2017.

The next room held a woman, in an even worse state. One eye was closed, the other stared wildly into the glass panel; she seemed oblivious to my presence. She too had been here for nearly three years — she was Sarah 2018.

I dropped the gun and ran, ignoring the searing pain in my chest and leg as I searched one room after another for my Anna. Each held a ruined human, the charts on the doors telling of the combination of experimental drugs and surgery used on them, and the results obtained; none of which had done anything more than halt the virus, at the cost of most of the patients senses.

Those towards the end of the hall were bald, fresh scars dissecting their heads. I found patient 2026 in the last room, and lost what little remained of the man I was.

I stumbled into the room and fell by her side. She looked past me with eyes glazed; her skin was pale, near translucent and her mouth hung open slightly. I ran a trembling hand over the scar running from the front of her shaved head to the back.

"Anna," I sobbed. I held her hand to my face and called her name again and again, as if I might bring her back to me by sheer force of will.

She shuddered slightly and whimpered, though still she looked through me, her hand limp in mine. I reached out and pulled her to my chest, kissing her and whispering softly, begging her to come back to me, though in my heart I knew she never could.

She whimpered slightly as I picked her up, and again as I carried her down the hall and out onto the grass. The sky was laced with pink fire; morning had come, and I headed for the upturned car with my wife cradled to me. She was light in my arms, lighter than any woman should be, but she was still beautiful, perfect. I lay her down for a moment to retrieve the bag from the smoking wreck of the old Ford, still on its side by the stairs.

No one tried to stop me.

The sun had cleared the mountains and was streaming golden light upon us as I carried her through the smashed gates and down the road. The light was warm, and tingled the skin. It had been years, since I was a child, that I relished the warmth of the sun so. Always it had been something to be avoided, feared even, but no longer. I turned east out

198

of instinct, the gold of the sun drawing me through the waking woods.

The burden of life I had so long carried, lifted from my being as I stumbled through the cool forest.

All of my scheming and planning, my stubbornness and ambition, everything I had held dear, or had thought important, had shrunk to insignificance without her. She was everything to me, and I prayed that she knew it. I whispered to her as I walked, told her that I would have done anything for her, that we would have been good parents, if only I had given us the chance.

In time my legs gave out and I collapsed in a sunny glade under a large oak. I was exhausted, my lungs on fire. I wiped at my mouth and stared uncaring at the dark streak of blood covering the back of my hand.

I rested against the trunk of the oak and held Anna's head to my chest, kissing her and whispering all the things I should said have when it mattered.

I don't know how long we sat together before I gave her five of the vials of serum I had brought from the zone. I prayed they would be enough. The other three I kept for myself. I flinched as I injected the first into my vein — I felt nothing by the time the third had been emptied.

The sun was warm and the sky blue. A slight breeze whispered through the leaves above us, sending gold dancing across her face. She was beautiful, she was my Anna, and she let out her last breath on my neck with a soft sigh.

I kissed her one last time before I too closed my eyes, and we slept together in the dappled sunlight of the forest, as she had always said she dreamed of us doing.

EPILOGUE

I buried her there in the forest.

I dug with sticks and then my hands. I buried her with the blue scarf and what few tears I had left. I wandered through the woods a shadow, many times I fell and somehow pushed myself to my feet.

In time the trees gave way to a farm.

Two small children stared wide-eyed as I emerged from the woods; the living dead. Their parents had left the world to make their own life in the mountains. They lived as Anna and I dreamed we might, when done with the city and ambition. The children were happy and free, and when I heard them playing outside as I lay recovering it broke my heart.

The couple asked me to stay, to live and to work with them. They told me there would soon be nothing left in the east, that cities were the death of mankind.

I left for the city as soon as I was able. I had nowhere else to go, and I became desperate to see my mother and brothers, who I had so selfishly abandoned. When I returned I found the world I had known, falling to pieces. The precarious apathy that had held it together for so long was no longer able to sustain its own weight, and the entire facade came crashing down around a populace waking from generations of slumber.

It was the memory of Anna that kept me alive in those dark times. I soon realized that my actions were futile, that she was lost to me the moment they took her — I should have accepted her fate and spared those still left to me the suffering my actions caused, as Anna would have wanted.

I only hope that after reading this, you might look to those dear to you and hold them closer. And perhaps, you might speak of my Anna to others, so that she won't be forgotten. So that when we, and all who knew us in life are gone, there will be someone in the world who remembers we even existed at all.